KUNDALINI CONSPIRACY

Andrew May

Post-Fortean Books

www.andrew-may.com

KUNDALINI CONSPIRACY

Copyright © 2000, 2004 by Andrew May

An earlier and substantially different version of this book appeared as a series of short stories in the webzine *Nuketown*, as follows:

"Feng Shui Abduction" (September 2000)
"Kundalini Conspiracy" (October 2000)
"Homicidal Homeopathy" (November 2000)
"Chaos Magic" (December 2000)

All rights reserved. No part of this publication may be reproduced, stored in a retrieval system, or transmitted, in any form or by any means, electronic, mechanical, photocopying, recording or otherwise, without the prior permission of the publisher and/or author, nor be otherwise circulated in any form of binding or cover other than that in which it is published and without a similar condition being imposed on the subsequent purchaser.

All characters in this publication are fictitious, and any resemblance to real persons, living or dead, is purely coincidental.

While every precaution has been taken in the preparation of this book, the publisher assumes no responsibilities for errors or omissions, or for damages resulting from the use of information contained herein.

Published by

Post-Fortean Books

www.andrew-may.com

CONTENTS

(1) THE MYSTIC MALL 4
(2) SEX AND SCIENCE 8
(3) ALIEN ABDUCTION 12
(4) ENCOUNTER WITH AN ELEMENTAL 15
(5) GRABBED BY THE GOVERNMENT 20
(6) KUNDALINI KAPERS 25
(7) ESCAPE FROM THE ENEMY 30
(8) FORTEAN FOOTWORK 35
(9) HOODOO HOMICIDE 39
(10) A RELUCTANT RECRUIT 43
(11) KINKY KARMA 46
(12) TESLA TECHNOLOGY 50
(13) PYRAMID POWER 55
(14) THOUSANDS OF THEORIES 58
(15) STANDING STONES 63
(16) ORAL ORACLE 67
(17) THE GOTHIC GURU 71
(18) NIGHT-TIME NECROMANCY 74
(19) A RAUNCHY RITUAL 77
(20) CONQUERING CHAOS 80

1

THE MYSTIC MALL

People call me a dismal loser, but the truth is that I have a rare talent. Like Charles Fort, Immanuel Velikovsky and Erich von Daniken before me, I have an uncanny ability to see through the plodding banality of everyday life to the great vistas of weirdness that lie beyond. Not everyone has a gift like that, and I finally realized it was my duty to apply my skills to the good of the community. I decided to turn professional.

I looked again at the small card I'd produced on my home computer. *Byron Bland, investigator of the Paranormal, the Unexplained and the generally Weird. No job too small, rates negotiable.* That would bring the work pouring in, especially in a quirky place like Blastonbury. This corner of rural England was a veritable nexus of weirdness, with more than its fair share of hauntings, crop circles, cattle mutilations and UFO sightings. And I knew exactly where to put the card to reach the kind of market I was looking for.

The Mystic Mall was an old Victorian courtyard in the heart of Blastonbury that had been taken over by a number of New Age businesses. There was a psychic bookshop, a health food store, a place that sold crystals and several other shops of that kind. I liked to hang around the Mystic Mall for two reasons: (a) because it was a magnet for the weirdness to which my life was dedicated, and (b) because the clientele was largely made up of kinky-looking women who merited close scrutiny. Some of them were well into middle-age, and many of them were overweight, but their kinkiness was beyond dispute. There was a preponderance of tattoos and body piercings, and a distinct preference for black clothes and silver jewelry. I could stand and watch them all day long.

At the center of the Mystic Mall was a Victorian Gothic meeting room, where public lectures on New Age subjects were held every Tuesday evening. Today was a Tuesday, but it just said *Speaker and subject to be announced*. Next week's lecture, however, was going to be a major event -- *Chaos Theory and Sacred Resonance*, by none other than Nik Shaman. Dr Shaman was a New Age celebrity, having written several books and appeared on TV. It was rare for him to appear in public outside London, and I made a prominent note of the event in my diary.

In the entry porch of the meeting room there was a large bulletin board. That's where I was going to put my card, in among all the ads for Tarot readers, aromatherapists, clairvoyants and Reiki practitioners. *Byron Bland, investigator of the Paranormal...*.

The glass window covering the bulletin board was locked. There was a small note in the corner saying *Key with Eric and Val*. Eric and Val Moonblade were the proprietors of the Mystic Mall's health food store, and the organizers of the Tuesday evening lectures. Eric was a tall, bony man with long, wild hair and unkempt beard, while Val was a short, plump woman with large breasts and close-cropped hair. The physical disparity between them led to some interesting speculations about their sex life. I tried to visualize dumpy little Val bouncing up and down on top of Eric's elongated body. They probably went in for kinky sex magic, Aleister Crowley style.

I went into the health food store. Val Moonblade was plumped on the stool behind the counter, dressed in a long floral skirt and yin-yang T-shirt. Her hair was dyed an unnaturally bright shade of orange, and from the relaxed shape of her bosom it was obvious she wasn't wearing a bra. I nodded inwardly to myself -- there was no doubt this was a very kinky woman.

She looked up at me. "Oh, hello -- your name's Byron, isn't it? What can I do for you today?"

"I'd like to borrow the key for your bulletin board," I said, ogling her breasts. "So I can pin my card up. I'm a paranormal investigator, you see." I showed her the card.

"Oh, how interesting!" she said. She rummaged through a drawer, breasts jiggling, and handed me the key. "I saw a UFO last week."

"Really?" I took out my notebook and pen. "That's exactly the sort of thing I ought to be investigating. Can you give me some details?"

"Well, it happened last Thursday evening," she said. "It was dark -- about eight o'clock, I think. I was driving along minding my own business, when I suddenly realized there was this light bobbing around in the sky ahead of me. I stopped the car and watched it. It swooped about for a few seconds, then disappeared."

I scribbled away in my notebook. "Whereabouts was this, exactly?" I asked.

"Oh, right out in the middle of nowhere," she said. "Near that old disused airfield."

I looked up. "You mean RAF Ovalon?" I said. "Not everyone believes that's as disused as the government says it is. It's still guarded by dogs and fenced off with razor wire, you know. There may be all sorts of top secret projects going on inside. Perhaps that's what your UFO was."

"Oh, I don't think so," Val said, shaking her head. "It didn't move like any earthly craft. And anyway, I know exactly where the UFO came from. I had a vision."

"A vision? I asked. I was still having visions of her in bed with Eric.

"Yes, I'm psychic," she explained. "After I saw the UFO I had a mystic vision in which a shining angel appeared and told me that the UFO had come to bring love and light to planet Earth. The angel said the UFO came from a star system called Capella."

"Oh, of course -- Crapellia!" I said, nodding knowingly. "Earth has had a lot of visits from the Crapellians, recently. They're one of the more benign races in the Galaxy. There's nothing to worry about." Actually, I'd never heard of the place before, but it's important for a paranormal investigator to put witnesses at their ease.

I went and pinned my card to the bulletin board, then returned the key to Val.

"Are you coming to the lecture tonight?" she asked.

"I don't know," I said. "What's it about?"

"It's called *Sex and Science in Ancient India*," Val said. "By Jishnu Mitra, a lecturer from Blastonbury College. We didn't advertize the title because we didn't want to attract the wrong sort of people. Because of the word sex, I mean."

"Very wise," I said. "You can't be too careful -- the world is full of perverts. But the science part sounds like it's right up my street. I'll be there."

2

SEX AND SCIENCE

The meeting room started to fill with people. A good three quarters of the audience was female, and I ogled them all carefully, choosing an appropriate one to sit next to. Finally I settled on a short, mousy-haired specimen dressed in a well-worn karate suit. The tight fitting, off-white fabric emphasized her gluteus maximus in a way that was totally irresistible. I sat down next to her.

At the front of the hall, Eric Moonblade was introducing the speaker."... all the way from Blastonbury College, to tell us about *Sex and Science in Ancient India*. Ladies and gentlemen, please welcome Jishnu Mitra." There was a burst of applause and Eric returned to his seat.

All eyes turned to Jishnu Mitra. He was a small, intense-looking young man, dressed smartly in a sports jacket and tie -- not the usual New Age type at all. As soon as he started to speak, it was obvious that he was an academic researcher holding forth on his specialist subject.

"The Indian civilization that I want to talk about is the great empire known as Rama, which flourished more than ten thousand years ago," Jishnu began. "As we shall see during the course of the lecture, the civilization of Rama was far in advance of our own in terms of science, technology, spirituality and the sexual arts."

I glanced at the mousy-haired young thing sitting next to me, and tried to visualize her indulging in advanced sexual arts. I looked to see if she was wearing a wedding ring, although it wouldn't have been an insurmountable obstacle to true lust even if she were married. However, she had rings on all her fingers and both thumbs, so it was impossible to tell. As I looked her over I saw she also had several rings in her ears and one in her pert little nose. She was some kind of kinky fetishist, obviously. I ogled the small bumps under the tight-fitting jacket of her karate suit, wondering if her nipples were pierced as well. I decided they probably were.

"In its day, Rama was one of the two great cultures in the world," Jishnu was saying. "One of the two great super-powers, to use the modern term. There was Rama in the East, and Atlantis in the west. Both cultures possessed advanced technology, but only Rama matched technological accomplishment with spiritual attainment. That is the reason why we know so much more about Rama today than we do about Atlantis. Spiritual echoes from the great minds of Rama still resonate through the astral dimensions, and these echoes can be picked up and channelled back into our continuum by psychically sensitive individuals."

Jishnu asked someone at the back of the room to turn the lights down so he could show some slides. The dimmer light came as a relief to me, as Karate Girl was starting to give me an erection with her kinky nipple rings and everything. I put my hand in my pocket and squeezed gently.

Jishnu's first slide showed the cover of a rather poorly produced book. "This is the bible of my subject," he said. "As you can see it's called *Yantras, or Mechanical Contrivances in Ancient India*, and it was written by Dr V. Raghavan in 1952. By collating writings from a variety of sources, Dr Raghavan was able to reveal for the first time the vast scale of ancient Indian technology. Flying machines, automobiles, robots, video phones... you name it, the Rama Empire had it. Dr Raghavan's most famous source was the *Vimanika Shastra*, a technical manual describing the Rama Empire's great flying machines or vimanas. Each vimana was equipped with a whole array of smaller machines or yantras, each with a specific purpose of its own...."

Jishnu started to click rapidly through a series of slides that depicted one weird-looking machine after another. There were radar yantras and stealth yantras, telecommunications yantras, death-ray yantras and tractor-beam yantras.

Finally Jishnu came to the end of the slides, and asked for the lights to be turned up. I blinked and took my hand out of my pocket. By this time I had a full erection, which I tried to hide by folding my hands in my lap.

"You may be wondering where the power for all these yantras came from," Jishnu said. "Did it come from the sun, or from coal, or from oil, or from nuclear energy? Well, it was none of these. The sages of ancient Rama used Kundalini energy, which is more powerful and more fundamental than any of the other sources I just mentioned. The nearest equivalent in modern science is the concept of the Zero-Point field -- the almost limitless energy latent in the very fabric of space itself. The sages of Rama developed several methods of raising Kundalini energy and exploiting it for their purposes. May I ask if any of you in the audience are familiar with the practices of Tantric Sex?"

Several of the women in the audience raised their hands, including mousy little Karate Girl. I raised my hand too. I'd only vaguely heard of Tantric Sex, but I didn't want to be left out if he was going to ask for volunteers.

"Then you will be aware that Kundalini energy is a deep and powerful form of sexual energy," Jishnu said. "It is present in semen, and can be raised by sexual intercourse or masturbation."

Masturbation was something I could really relate to! I grabbed my crotch, Michael Jackson style, and turned to the girl sitting next to me. I looked right into her eyes but she pretended not to see me. She kept on looking straight ahead. I rubbed my crotch anyway.

"Sex is only one aspect of Kundalini energy," Jishnu said. "It goes much further than that. In the days of the Rama empire, Kundalini energy was everything -- spiritual, psychic, technological... it was the fundamental science of its time. Kundalini energy provided the power source for all the different yantras I was talking about earlier."

I grunted as I ejaculated in my jeans. Karate Girl shifted in her seat, leaning further away from me. At last, an acknowledgement of my existence! She probably fancied me like mad. I speculated on some of the Tantric sex practices we would get up to together.

I was still speculating when it dawned on me that the lecture was over and the audience had begun to applaud. I joined in the applause, then rose to make my way out of the meeting room. I looked around, but the mousy-haired, multiply pierced Karate Girl had disappeared.

3

ALIEN ABDUCTION

The sun was setting by the time I got on my bicycle and started to make my way home. It wasn't a long journey -- just half a mile to the edge of Blastonbury, then another couple of miles along a winding lane to the little village where I lived. As I rode along I descended into a daydream. My mind started to swirl with thoughts of ancient Indian flying machines, Tantric sex practices, kinky New Age women and aliens from Capella. Weird, weird, weird. I thought back to the ad I'd placed on the bulletin board in the Mystic Mall: *Byron Bland, paranormal investigator....* With so much weirdness around, it wouldn't be long before the work started to roll in.

The road wound past Dogbarrow Hill, with its prehistoric burial mound and mysterious stone circle. It was too dark to see either the hill or the prehistoric relics, but in my mind they simply added to the catalogue of local weirdness. There had been rumors in the press about a strange cult that met in darkness on the summit of the hill and did... well, things. The papers weren't specific as to what sort of things, but there was little doubt in my mind that they were sexual things. It's always the same with these strange, mysterious cults -- wild, frenzied, naked dancing, and uninhibited sexual orgies. I could visualize it clearly in my mind's eye.

As I continued to cycle along the deserted road I began to get the strange feeling that I wasn't alone. Maybe the road wasn't so deserted after all. I looked around. There was nothing on the road behind me, or ahead of me. Then I saw it. There was some kind of light -- not on the road itself, but moving along parallel to it, on the opposite side from Dogbarrow Hill. The light was intermittently visible through the trees. It looked as if it was floating above ground level.

This was it, I thought -- the real thing! There was no other explanation at this time of night. It had to be a UFO. An alien spaceship -- possibly the same one that Val Moonblade saw, from Capella or wherever it was. Or maybe this was from somewhere else, like Zeta Reticuli or the Pleiades. If only I had my camera... but of course no-one had their camera with them when they saw a real UFO. Only hoaxers had cameras. I stood and watched the UFO with growing amazement as it darted and swooped about in a totally unearthly manner. Then it came to a halt and I realized with a shock that it had seen me -- or rather its occupants had seen me. I'd shown up on their infra-red scanners, without doubt. And now they were debating what to do about me. After a few moments, the light started to move again. It drifted toward me until it was directly overhead.

Belatedly I began to wonder if stopping on a deserted stretch of road to watch the UFO had been such a good idea after all. I made to get back on my bicycle and found that I was incapable of movement. I was completely paralyzed from head to foot! A moment later I was bathed in a beam of white light, and levitated gently into the strange vehicle hovering overhead.

When I regained consciousness I was lying on a shiny metal examination table in a brightly lit room, beneath a domed metallic ceiling. I was stark naked and held firmly in place by steel restraints around my arms, legs and forehead. I'd read enough about UFOs and alien abductions to know exactly what was going on here. Well, the aliens had picked the wrong person this time. They hadn't reckoned on Byron Bland, paranormal investigator!

Two figures were bending over me, dressed in shiny gray spacesuits with mirror-glass helmets that hid their features. Aliens, obviously. They were busy probing me all over with some rather nasty looking gadgets. I had the feeling they were making electrical measurements of some kind. Whatever it was, I wasn't going to put up with it.

"This is degrading and obscene," I shouted. "What you're doing is an abomination in the eyes of all civilized beings in the galaxy. It's against all natural and ethical laws. I know my rights. And if I...."

There was a sudden shriek, originating somewhere over to my left. Then a female voice, saying something like "Oh, *men, really!*" This was followed by a whirring sound, then a slithering sound, then a distant plonking sound, and then silence.

I turned my head with difficulty, and could just make out a second, now empty, examination table a few feet to the left of mine. I dimly wondered what the *whirr - slither - plonk* sound could have signified. Then the aliens finished their probing, and the metal restraints snapped open. I started to jump up, but as soon as I did so the foot of the table whirred upwards to a steep angle, and I found myself slithering backwards down a chute leading to some lower level of the strange vessel. I was deposited with an unceremonious plonk on the floor of a tiny cell. *Whirr - slither - plonk...* just like that!

4

ENCOUNTER WITH AN ELEMENTAL

From my vantage point on the floor, I caught my first glimpse of the source of the female voice. Obviously she'd been the occupant of the other examination table, and had been deposited in the cell a few moments before me. By the time I arrived she had raised herself up to her full height (all five feet of it), and was busy dusting herself down. Like myself, the aliens had stripped her naked. My eyes moved up her body, taking in the chunky thighs, wide hips, narrow waist, taut stomach and cheeky little breasts. Her pert-nosed face was surrounded by a dishevelled halo of mousy brown hair.

"It's you!" I shouted. "Karate Girl! Hey babe, it's your lucky day. Bet you never thought you'd see me again so soon."

She looked blankly at me for a few seconds before recognition set in. "Oh, the filthy little toad who was masturbating during the lecture," she said. "I'd forgotten." She took a step back and a strange expression came over her face, as though she had an unpleasant pain in her stomach. This was an effect I had on women sometimes -- I put it down to sexual chemistry.

I looked at her some more. Her body was firm and athletic, if somewhat bottom-heavy. Her pubic mound was completely shaven, with the image of a snake tattooed on it. She had jeweled rings piercing both nipples, just as I'd imagined. And she had another piercing as well.

"You've got a ring in your clitoris," I said, trying to sound gallant. "I think I'm in love. What's your name?"

"I'm Jessica Peace-Lily, Master of advanced Celtic Yogic Feng Shui," she said, looking back at me with two big eyes and two little nostrils. "I'm a Tantric Elemental, black belt 9th Dan with three purple stripes."

"That's a lot of talent in a small package," I observed. "My name's Byron Bland, and I'm a paranormal investigator. I've done loads of research on oriental beliefs and all that New Age stuff, so I know what those words mean that you just used. Most of them, anyway. I read a book about Feng Shui which went on about five-element theory. You know -- Water, Wood, Fire, Earth and uh, Metal."

There was a sound as the hatch in the ceiling of the cell slid open again. Two bundles of clothes plopped to the floor -- first hers, then mine. The aliens wanted us to get dressed.

Jessica turned to her clothes and knelt down to sort through them. She had her back to me now, which gave me an unfettered opportunity to admire her magnificent butt. There was certainly a lot of it to admire. A gluteus maximus with the emphasis on maximus. I started to get an erection.

"We're in quite a fix," Jessica was saying. "We've been abducted by aliens and we don't know what they're going to do next. It's serious, but there must be a way out. Perhaps five-element theory is just what we need." She turned to look at me. She saw my erection and wrinkled her nose. "Well, you're obviously a Woody type, for a start."

"Thank you," I said modestly. I picked up my jeans and started to pull them on.

"As for me, I represent the Earth element," Jessica continued. "I can see from the direction of your gaze that you've already noticed I'm wearing the symbol of mother Earth."

With a start, I realized that the rather fetching tattoo nestled between her pert little breasts was none other than the Chinese pictograph for Earth.

"Yes, they're lovely," I agreed.

Jessica finished squeezing into her tight little karate suit, securing the low-necked top with a frayed and much-worn black belt. "Most important of all, these horrible aliens are Metal types," she was saying. "Their ship and instruments are all metal. And the silvery gray spacesuits, the incessant probing and analysis... they're all Metal characteristics."

"Yep," I contributed, helpfully.

"Now, as I'm sure your book told you, Fire controls Metal. So you can see what that means."

"Right -- we torch the joint," I said, pleased that I could keep up with her reasoning.

Jessica shook her head. "No, not that. In oriental terms, Fire energy encompasses more than just physical fire. It also has an important spiritual aspect. And that's what's going to save us. We must get spiritual."

"How about a bit of spiritual sex?" I said, cottoning on quickly. "You said you were a Tantric Elephantic or something. That was in the lecture tonight -- Tantric sexual practices. Let's do some of that mystical shagging."

"I don't think so," Jessica said. "I've seen your penis and it's too small. I'm a high-order Tantric adept and I've got standards." She wrinkled her nose again. "No, what we must do is meditate. That will be our route to salvation." With a single practised motion she adopted the lotus posture.

Figuratively scraping myself off the soles of her pretty little feet, I followed her example.

Jessica began to chant: "As we read in the Visuddhimagga, chapter 12, verse 87. *Seated cross-legged, they travel through space like winged birds. They go unhindered through walls, as though through open space. To do this they should first enter the space-perception trance, and then emerging from it they should focus on the wall. They should resolve 'Let there be space', and the wall shall become as space. Then they will be able to pass through unhindered.*"

What happened next was the weirdest thing so far. After several minutes of chanting, our bodies gently lifted off the ground and began to drift slowly through the wall of the cell. We passed through other parts of the strange vessel, through rooms containing outlandish machinery, along narrow corridors and up and down lift shafts. I'd never seen anything like it! Jessica might have been small and mousy, but she clearly had supernatural talents almost as unique as my own. There was little doubt the two of us were made for each other.

Eventually we materialized in what appeared to be the control room of the craft. In front of us, two spacesuited figures sat side by side facing a viewscreen, while two others stood in front of control panels on the left and right sides of the room. The aliens looked around in astonishment as we made our entrance.

"What now?" I asked.

"Now we kick some alien ass," Jessica said, smashing together the heads of the two seated aliens. She turned to the alien on the right. "Abduct this!" she suggested, kicking him violently on the chin. The alien fell back against the far wall.

I started to look around the control room for some kind of vase or flower pot, with the vague notion of dropping it on the head of the fourth alien. But as I stepped forward I tripped over one of the fallen aliens and fell headlong on the floor. Just at that moment, a door slid open and two more aliens entered. They were both holding pistol-like blaster weapons. Jessica bent over the slumped body of the first alien, whipped the blaster from his belt and fired straight at the line of aliens, knocking down not only the two new ones but also the original one standing beyond them.

"That was lucky," Jessica said. "This appears to be a relatively unsophisticated single-shot weapon, designed to stun an opponent. It's a good thing you ducked when you did, or I wouldn't have got a clear line to all three of them."

"Yes, we make a great team," I agreed, beaming at her.

Jessica eased the alien commander off his chair and sat down, studying the controls thoughtfully. I sat next to her and looked up at the viewscreen. Hundreds of tiny white dots drifted slowly towards us.

"Look at all those stars," I said. "How will we ever find our way home?"

"Oh that's just their screen saver," Jessica said, nudging the alien equivalent of a mouse. The screen cleared to show a view of the English countryside, seen from an altitude of a few hundred feet. The ship appeared to be drifting over the landscape at little more than walking pace.

"That's more like it!" I said. "You know a lot, don't you? Where did you learn to fly spaceships and float through walls and all that stuff?"

Jessica turned back toward me. "I already told you -- I'm a Tantric Elemental and a Master of advanced Celtic Yogic Feng Shui." she said. She looked me up and down. "And you're just a shabby little man with a small dick. For the life of me I can't imagine why the aliens were interested in you."

Kundalini Conspiracy

5

GRABBED BY THE GOVERNMENT

There was a sudden movement in the corner. A voice said: "It will all become clear in time, my dear."

Jessica and I exchanged a brief "uh oh" glance, and then turned to look at the source of the voice. One of the aliens had recovered enough to pick himself up off the floor.

"And one other thing," he said, fumbling with the catch on the mirror-glass space helmet. "We're not aliens." He removed the helmet to reveal a perfectly normal-looking crew-cut young man. "As you can see, I'm as human as you are. Probably more so, since I have the honor of working for Her Majesty's government. Allow me to introduce myself -- I'm Flight Lieutenant Simon Scimitar of the Royal Air Force."

Scimitar picked up one of the stun weapons and covered us with it as he went over to the control panel and made some adjustments. "We'll be landing shortly," he said.

Looking at the viewscreen, I suddenly realized where we were heading. It could be nowhere else but RAF Ovalon, the supposedly disused local airbase. This confirmed all my theories! I'd never seriously believed the government's story about the closure of the airbase. Deep beneath the innocuous aircraft shelters on the surface, there was obviously still a sophisticated underground complex which the government used for its most secret projects. That's why it was still protected by a razor-wire fence and guard dogs. The present circumstances weren't exactly ideal, but at least I was finally going to get inside the fence and see what was really going on!

By the time we touched down on the airfield, the sun was rising into a blue sky. The abduction experience must have lasted all night. Subjectively it hadn't seemed like it, but that was only to be expected. "Missing time" is always a factor in this sort of situation.

As we emerged from the vehicle we had been in, I had my first opportunity to examine it clearly from the outside. It was golden in color, and shaped like a huge church bell. It must have been at least a hundred feet in diameter at the base, and getting on for fifty feet high. My first good look at a real UFO, and to think I'd actually been inside it!

Scimitar escorted us across the tarmac toward the largest of the base's hardened aircraft shelters. As we approached, I discerned a large figure "18" over the main doors.

"I always knew you kept captured UFOs here," I remarked smugly.

"There are no UFOs at this site," Scimitar said without looking at me.

"What do you call that then?" I pointed back at the huge vehicle we'd just emerged from.

"It's not a UFO," Scimitar said. I began to recognize his tactics for what they were. A stonewall... an official denial. Obviously we were onto something big! I looked back at Jessica, but she was just tagging along quietly. She looked rather bored.

We entered the hangar. It housed an incomplete vehicle of a similar design to the one outside. Dozens of men in green coveralls were swarming over the craft, working on it.

"There's another one!" I said. "You're obviously back-engineering these UFOs from alien plans you retrieved from some crash site or other. This sort of thing happens all the time in America."

Scimitar stopped in his tracks and turned on me. "Look, will you get it into your head once and for all -- these aren't UFOs

Kundalini Conspiracy Page 21

and they've got nothing to do with aliens." He resumed walking toward the far side of the hangar.

We came to an elevator and the Flight Lieutenant ushered us in. He pressed a button and we began to descend. "But you're right about one thing," he continued. "The vehicles are back-engineered, all right. It's just that they're not UFOs. They're vimanas, ancient Indian flying machines. The ones we're recreating were designed during the Rama Empire more than ten thousand years ago."

"Oh, I know all about vimanas," I said. "So does my friend Jessica here. We went to a lecture on the subject. But you're still getting help from the aliens, aren't you? You need them to show you how to build it, because they've been visiting Earth for millennia and they know more about our ancient civilizations than we do."

Scimitar glared at me. "No aliens," he said.

The elevator continued to descend for several seconds.

"And I'm not his friend," Jessica said.

Eventually the elevator came to a halt and we emerged into a spacious and lavishly furnished lobby. Scimitar led the way down a corridor to the left, after swiping a card to open the access door.

"A lot of the technical details about vimanas can be found in ancient Sanskrit texts," he said. "Old technical manuals such as the *Vimanika Shastra*. To fill in the gaps, we use a form of past-life regression. That's where you come in. Our initial probes revealed that you both had some involvement with vimanas in a previous life. The Wing Commander will explain the rest to you."

We stopped in front of a door marked *Wing Commander Aden Adastra, Commander-in-Chief Back Engineering Group*. Scimitar knocked, stuck his head round the door and said a few words. Then he ushered us into the office, turned and left. Wing Commander Adastra greeted us and invited us to sit down.

Adastra was a large man with a shaven head and penetrating eyes. I shifted uncomfortably under his gaze. He produced a sheet of paper with a diagram on it -- a double spiral wound around a shaft surmounted by a pair of wings.

"Do either of you recognize this symbol?" he asked.

"Yes, of course," Jessica said. "It's the caduceus of Hermes. It represents the DNA molecule, the symbol of life. It's used as the emblem of the medical profession."

"Most people think that," Adastra said. "But DNA was only discovered 50 years ago. This symbol is much older -- one of the oldest symbols known to man. It holds the key to vimana technology. The spiral represents the coiled serpent Kundalini, the mystic channel through which the ancient Indians accessed the almost limitless energies of the Zero-Point field."

I nodded intelligently, though I was only half listening. I'd just noticed that, when Adastra leaned forward, I could see myself reflected in the smoothly polished top of his head. I started to pull what I thought was a series of amusing faces.

Adastra suddenly looked up and glared at me. "The wings symbolize the vimana's ability to fly. The central shaft provides the motive power. The sphere at the bottom is the mercury engine, and the one at the top is a crystal to focus the energy. Different crystals are used to achieve different effects. We've worked out what most of the crystals are and what they're for. But there's something in the ancient texts about a *Kalpaka* crystal. It's a particularly powerful crystal, with the effect of teleporting persons or objects instantaneously from one place to another. We want that crystal, but we don't know what it is. We need to know what *Kalpaka* means -- that's what we want you to find out for us."

Jessica frowned. "Why should we help you?" she asked. "I'm a pacifist -- I have a very low opinion of the military. You've abducted us and now you're telling us what to do."

Adastra looked at her. "You'll help us because you'll be helping yourselves at the same time," he said slowly. "By regressing to your former selves, you will find out more about Kundalini energy than you could ever possibly learn in the modern world. Among other things, Kundalini energy is sexual energy. We think that will appeal to you, both of you. We've studied you carefully, you know. So what do you say?"

"Sounds cool -- let's do it!" I said, without a moment's hesitation. Then I looked at Jessica. So did Adastra.

Jessica was silent for several seconds. "Okay, let's do it," she said finally.

"I'm sure you've both made the right decision," Adastra said. "Now, we're going to regress you back to a previous life during the ancient Rama Empire, some ten thousand years ago. At that time Rama was engaged in a long drawn-out war of attrition with Atlantis, but that's really as much as I can tell you at this stage. You'll have to pick up the rest as you go along."

Rising, Adastra picked up the gold-braided cap from the corner of his desk and put it on his head. He led us out of his office and along the corridor to a door marked *Regression Laboratory*. We followed him in.

The Wing Commander led us over to the regression machine, and a couple of technicians wired us up.

"It's all automated these days," Adastra was saying. "We don't use hypnosis any more -- it proved to be too unreliable. This machine will take care of everything. You'll be completely immersed in the world of the past. But remember your mission... remember to find out what the Kalpaka crystal is."

6

KUNDALINI KAPERS

I was standing in bright sunshine at the edge of a grassy airfield, dressed in oil-smeared coveralls and holding a toolbox. Ahead of me towered a larger version of the vimana that had abducted us. This one was at least twice the size, I estimated. My previous self knew the ship well -- she was the pride of Rama's Imperial Air Navy. In the distance beyond the airfield I could see the gleaming spires and pinnacles of Ayodhya, capital city of the Rama Empire. Nothing this side of Atlantis could match that fabulous skyline.

My reverie was broken by a coarse shout. "Airman Third Class Blandanovaka -- get your sorry ass up here at the double!" (this was spoken in Sanskrit, which was the only language my previous self understood).

I looked up to see Chief Petty Officer Hanuman glaring at me from the open hatch of the vimana. The Chief was a blue-faced monkey. I mean literally, that's what he was. Monkeys were a lot more intelligent in those days, and the blue-faced species in particular made excellent middle managers.

The Chief turned and disappeared into the vimana, his long prehensile tail curving out of a hole in the back of his coveralls. I hurried over to the ladder and started to ascend. This was an old ship, and I'd worked on her my whole career. I knew every inch of her like the back of my hand.

I went through the hatch into the dimly-lit interior. As I stepped inside I tripped over a thick cable, did a couple of somersaults, and ended up in a heap against the opposite bulkhead. I was slightly dazed, but it was pretty much where I'd been fixing to get to.

I picked up my toolbox and opened the access panel to the crystal yantra. I squeezed the upper part of my body inside the tight space in the midst of all the machinery and set to work. This was my job -- making sure all the crystals were freshly charged and fully functional. There were crystals for propulsion, sensors, communications, weapons and countermeasures. I had a full set of spares in my toolbox.

Suddenly I heard the Chief's voice cry out again. "Captain on the flight deck!"

I jumped up and hit my head with a sickening thud on the machinery above. I lay down for a few seconds, then propped myself up on one elbow and saluted.

"A thousand apologies, Captain," I said, peering through the spinning stars at the figure standing over me.

The Captain was Jessica. There was no doubt about it -- her previous self was almost identical to her modern one. She had the same deep tan and dark brown hair, and the same cute upturned nose and magnificently large butt. She was clad in a diaphanous silken robe that was so transparent that it revealed every detail of what she was wearing underneath. And that wasn't much -- just a skimpy black thong, high leather boots and virtually nothing else. Tight metal bands encircled her thighs and upper arms, and a beaded necklace dangled between her pert little breasts, but that was it. Hello, Captain! Officers certainly knew how to dress in the ancient Indian Imperial Air Navy.

"We need to get this crate in the air," Jessica said. "Two fully armed Atlantean vailix craft have just ingressed into our airspace west of Mohenjo Daro, and they're heading this way. Let's make them wish they'd stayed in bed."

Jessica installed herself in the Captain's seat. "All crew to action stations ready for launch," she said. "Okay, power up."

There was a growing hum as the mercury engine fired up, channeling the raw Kundalini energy of the Zero-Point field. It began HUMMMM-HUMMMM-HUMMMM, then changed to a clanging TRAM-TRAM-TRAM-TRAM, then a screeching HRIH-HRIH-HRIH, then a roaring AAAHHHH, and finally a deeply resonant OMMM-OMMM-OMMM.

Inside the crystal yantra in front of me, the main propulsion crystal glowed a dull throbbing red. The vimana lifted effortlessly off the ground, ascended several thousand feet, and then transitioned into level flight.

"Vector to intercept coordinates," Captain Jessica ordered. "Commence all-sensor search."

The pink Darapana crystal started to glow, and the screen lit up with the long-range view ahead of us. Within minutes, a tiny dot appeared in the cloudless sky, growing rapidly. A slender aluminum needle some two hundred feet long, it was the unmistakable form of an Atlantean attack vailix.

A sharply focused beam of light shot out of the vailix directly towards us.

"Activate the Pinjula shield," Jessica shouted. At the weapons console, Chief Hanuman flicked a switch and we were enveloped in a protective yellow glow. The Atlantean force beam hit the shield harmlessly.

"Launch Indra's Dart," Jessica ordered. The Chief turned a key and simultaneously pressed a button, and a high speed arrow shot toward the vailix, homing in on the sound it made. The Atlantean vessel attempted an evasive maneuver, but it was no match for the superior speed of the dart. There was a brief explosion, and the remains of the vailix plummeted to the ground.

"No sign of the other one -- he must be cloaked," Jessica said. "Well, we'll do the same. Deploy Maya."

The black Maya crystal glowed dully. Maya was the Sanskrit word for illusion -- it caused us to blend imperceptibly into the background. Modern stealth technology was nothing compared to Maya.

"Okay, let's get this over with," Captain Jessica said. "Activate the Nandaka crystal."

In front of me, the Nandaka crystal glowed green. By now, all hostile beings within its range of influence would be in a deep coma.

The second vailix craft shimmered into view. No sooner had it appeared than it started to glide gently down toward the arid landscape below. We watched on the viewscreen as the vailix bumped down in a rough landing. A cloud of dust billowed around it, but otherwise the vessel appeared to remain intact.

"Interesting," Jessica said. "There's obviously some sort of automatic recovery system fitted to that ship. I've never seen that before -- our technical people will want to take a look at it. And it means we'll be able to take a few prisoners this time." She turned to me. "Airman, teleport the Chief down so he can round up the survivors."

Chief Hanuman stepped onto the teleport pad and I activated the purple Kalpaka crystal. The Chief winked out of existence. We continued to hover over the crash site. Captain Jessica made a call back to base to tell them about the new design vailix. She passed on details of its location -- a specialist recovery team would be sent out for it later.

A few minutes later a chime sounded and the Kalpaka crystal started glowing again. The Chief reappeared on the teleport pad, together with three rather glum looking Atlanteans. The chief was covering them with a sonic rifle.

"Well done, Chief," Jessica said. "Escort the prisoners down to the cells. We'll set a course for home."

There wasn't much to do on the way back, so I settled down to read a technical manual. Well, that's how my previous self thought of it -- a Kundalini technical manual. Which I guess is what it was, but it wasn't all wiring diagrams and schematics. It was hot stuff.

Jishnu Mitra had been right when he said that Tantric sex and Kundalini were aspects of the same thing. Kundalini energy might come from the Zero-Point field or whatever it was called, but exactly the same force was present in semen. You could raise Kundalini with all these crystals and yantra gadgets, but you could also raise it by masturbating a lot. I could relate to that. I guess it made me something of an expert in Kundalini raising... and it meant I had an ability that no woman on her own could ever have. No wonder Jessica had such an obsession with huge dicks. It probably explained why she had a pubic snake tattoo, as well. She was trying to compensate for something she desperately wanted but could never have!

I read on. The manual talked about the Lingam, which was Sanskrit for penis, and Yoni, which was Sanskrit for pussy. But the terms Lingam and Yoni seemed to signify much more than the physical organs alone. A bit like the oriental concepts of Yin and Yang, they represented the fundamental male and female principles that drive everything that exists. The sacred union of male and female was called Yab-Yum, which as far as I could tell was a peculiar mystical form of sexual intercourse. I flicked through the pictures, masturbating openly because this was my previous self and masturbation was okay in those days. Everyone knew it was one of the best ways to raise Kundalini.

7

ESCAPE FROM THE ENEMY

Suddenly we were back at the airbase. The technicians were busy disconnecting us from the machine.

"Hey, I was just reading a good book!" I said. "What did you have to bring us back for?"

"You've had enough time to get the information the Wing Commander wanted," one of the technicians said. "It's time for your debriefing."

We were led back to Adastra's office. The Wing Commander immediately started to interrogate us.

"The teleport crystal, the one the texts call Kalpaka -- were you able to identify it?" Adastra leaned forward eagerly.

"I certainly was," I said smugly, pleased that I could show off my newly acquired technical knowledge. "It's the purple one."

Jessica raised her eyes to the ceiling. "In other words, amethyst," she said.

"Amethyst -- excellent," Adastra said, rubbing his hands. "That's all we need to know. We'll have that teleport device working in no time!"

Jessica and I stood up to leave.

"Ah, just one moment," Adastra said, looking slightly embarrassed. "We have a small security problem here. You see, this project is classified Top Secret, and I'm sure you'll understand that we can't risk a couple of civilians blabbing about it to all and sundry."

We sat down again, vaguely expecting some sort of financial inducement to keep our mouths shut.

"People disappear for no apparent reason all the time, don't they?" Adastra continued. "Especially unattached single people like the two of you. People who lead, ah, somewhat alternative lifestyles."

I grinned from ear to ear. Jessica was unattached and single! That left me free to pursue her without interference from husbands, boyfriends or the like. Then my smile gradually faded as it dawned on me that, in one interpretation at least, the Wing Commander's words could have been construed as a rather nasty threat.

Jessica slipped her hand inside the top of her karate suit, and a moment later produced a ring with a green gem embedded in it. She aimed it at Adastra, who slumped back in his chair, unconscious.

"My left nipple ring is an emerald," Jessica explained. "Otherwise known as a Nandaka crystal, as we've just learned. The one that renders hostile people unconscious. Let's get going -- he won't be out for long."

I didn't need telling twice. I followed Jessica into the corridor. Suddenly I stopped dead in my tracks. I was keen to get out of there, but I didn't want to leave empty handed, without some kind of hard evidence. I was a paranormal investigator, after all. I turned round and went back into Adastra's office.

Looking round for a suitable memento of the occasion, I grabbed the Wing Commander's gold-braided cap and put it on my head. As an afterthought I unclipped the name tag from his jacket, then turned and raced back into the corridor.

Panting for breath, I finally caught up with Jessica.

"Oh, do come on," she said. "We haven't got much time."

As we came to the end of the corridor an alarm bell started clanging.

"Damn," Jessica said. We were just a few feet from the elevator leading back up to the surface, but between us and it there was a locked door.

Jessica stared at me. I was still fumbling to clip Adastra's name tag onto my T-shirt.

"You're a genius!" she said, snatching the tag off me.

"Hey, that's mine!" I shouted. But I calmed down quickly -- after all, she'd finally acknowledged my superior intellect.

Jessica swiped the tag through the reader on the door and pushed it open. The name tag doubled as a swipe card -- a fact that my brain had no doubt deduced subconsciously, which is why I'd risked my life to go back and retrieve it.

It took an eternity for the elevator to arrive, and then another eternity for it to ascend to ground level. As the door opened, Flight Lieutenant Scimitar lunged at us. Jessica ducked down, took a little sideways skip, and made a graceful gesture with her hands. She made no physical contact with Scimitar, but he was knocked flat on his back as if he'd been hit by a freight train.

"Quick, into the vimana," Jessica said. A handful of men in green coveralls rushed out to stop us, but she dealt with them as effortlessly as she had with Scimitar. She ran up the ladder into the vimana, and I followed close behind her. As I stepped through the hatch into the darkness within, I tripped over exactly the same cable that I had ten thousand years ago. However, this being a smaller craft, I only completed one somersault before crashing into the opposite bulkhead. I sat rubbing my head.

"Quick, onto the teleport pad," Jessica ordered. "There's not much time."

"But their teleport doesn't work," I pointed out. "Not without one of those athemist crystals. They didn't even know it was supposed to be athemist until we told them."

"Amethyst," Jessica said, unclipping a purple earring. "I never go anywhere without one." She deftly inserted the crystal into its housing, then joined me on the teleport pad.

A second later we were somewhere else. A country lane -- the one near Dogbarrow Hill where I'd been abducted the previous evening. I could even see my bicycle lying by the side of the road where I'd left it.

"That was pretty cool, the way you dealt with Scimitar and the others back there," I said, putting on the peaked cap I'd retrieved from the Wing Commander's office. I adjusted it to what I thought was a jaunty angle.

"Oh, that was nothing," Jessica said. "Just basic aikido -- anyone can learn to do it. Almost anyone, I mean." She looked me up and down. Then she did a double take. "That's odd," she said. "Let me take a closer look at that cap."

I took the cap off and handed it to her. "No funny stuff," I warned. "I want it back -- it's evidence."

Jessica inspected the cap and gave it back to me. "You're right," she said. "It is evidence. Evidence that there's more to what just happened than meets the eye. Look at the cap badge."

"It's a pyramid with an eye in it," I said. "So what?"

"Well, I'm not an expert on RAF cap badges, but I'm pretty sure that's not one of them." Jessica frowned thoughtfully. "Whoever those people were working for, it wasn't the government. The government is sinister enough, but I think this is worse. It's some kind of independent force, possibly a supernatural one. We need to be careful."

"Good idea," I said. "Let's be careful together. I live just around the corner -- how about a cup of coffee? Adastra said you were single and unattached, so there's nothing to stop you."

Jessica looked at me. "I've got a better idea," she said. "You give me the creeps -- I don't want to see you ever again. If you try to come within two hundred yards of me, I'll take out a court order against you." She started walking back toward the town.

I stood there for a few moments, then shouted after her. "I've got you all worked out," I yelled. "You're compensating because you haven't got a lingummy thingummy and you wish you had!"

Kundalini Conspiracy

I thought I saw her hesitate for a moment, but she didn't turn round. I watched her until she disappeared along the winding lane.

8

FORTEAN FOOTWORK

With or without Ms Jessica Peace-Lily, I was determined to get to the bottom of whatever it was that was going on at the disused airbase. The people there were obviously doing something very sinister. First they'd posed as aliens and abducted us. Then they'd pretended to be government officials and used us like pawns in some kind of time travel experiment. Finally they'd threatened to get rid of us permanently. I wasn't sure what their game was, but I didn't like it.

Given the razor wire and guard dogs, there was no way I was going to get back into the airbase. But there were other ways of finding things out. Charles Fort, the first and greatest of all paranormal investigators, spent a lifetime searching through local newspapers for the smallest signs of weirdness. He uncovered all sorts of mysteries that way, tucked away in minor news items from around the world. So I decided to follow in Fort's footsteps and scour the last few weeks' worth of local papers for anything out of the ordinary.

My search turned up quite a few UFO sightings, which in retrospect were almost certainly attributable to the back-engineered vimana from the airbase. In fact, now I came to think of it, that probably explained Val Moonblade's sighting as well. Despite her conviction that it came from the star system of Capella, or whatever it was she said the angel had told her.

Then I found something that really caught my attention, tucked away on an inside page of one of the papers from a few weeks ago. The item was headed *Servants of Thoth*, and it was about the mysterious cult that was supposed to hold rituals on the summit of Dogbarrow Hill. According to the article, the cult was gaining new members all the time. It quoted Reverend Titus Odling, the vicar at Saint Diana's church in Blastonbury, as saying "Thoth is the devil, and the servants of Thoth are servants of the devil."

It seemed to be worth following up. The way I looked at it, there were two possibilities. Either the Servants of Thoth would turn out to be the sinister force behind the goings on at the airbase, or else my original assumption was correct and they were just another harmless sex cult. If the former, then that would solve the case for me. If the latter, then I could join the cult and take part in all the orgies and stuff. Either way it would be a good deal.

The best lead I had on the cult was the vicar, Titus Odling, so I decided to pay him a visit. I cycled into Blastonbury and parked my bicycle outside Saint Diana's church. It was a big, gloomy mediaeval building in the Gothic style. I went inside and found Reverend Odling working in a side office.

"Hi, my name's Byron Bland," I said, flashing my library card at him by way of identification. "I'm a paranormal investigator."

"Really? How fascinating!" Reverend Odling said, looking up from his work. "How may I help you?" He was younger than I'd expected, with big glasses and a round face.

"I'm interested in finding out more about the cult," I said.

"Which cult? There are so many in Blastonbury, you know."

"The Servants of Thoth," I said.

"Oh, that cult," he said. "A very religious group of people, if I may say so."

His answer took me by surprise. "But in the paper you were quoted as saying they were evil."

He looked shocked. "I'm sure I didn't say that. I would never say anything so judgmental."

"You said that Thoth was the devil, and the servants of Thoth were servants of the devil."

"Oh, I may have said that," the vicar admitted. "But that's not the same thing as saying they're evil. The devil is just like God, only slightly different. Worshipping the devil is just as valid as worshipping God, these days."

"I didn't realize the church was so open-minded about that sort of thing," I said.

"This church is," he said. "Especially since we were rededicated to Saint Diana a few years ago. We're a lot more tolerant of little things like sin, sex and satanism these days."

I scribbled a few notes. "Getting back to the Servants of Thoth," I said. "Who or what is Thoth, exactly?"

"Thoth is our leader," Reverend Odling said. "The leader of the cult, I mean. The leader of the Servants of Thoth. I don't know why I said *our leader* just now."

"You mean he's a real person?" I asked. "Where does he live? What does he look like?"

"He's a real person, all right," the vicar said. "But I can't tell you who he is or what he looks like. He always wears a hooded robe and a mask. I mean, that's what the cult members have told me. I'm not a member myself, you understand."

I looked at him doubtfully. "I think I understand," I said. "But the name Thoth -- it's rather unusual. Where does it come from?"

"Thoth was the name of a god in ancient Egypt," he said.

"Ancient Egypt, as in pyramids?" I asked. There was a *click* inside my head as something fell into place.

"That's right," he said. "Thoth was the Egyptian equivalent of the Greek god Hermes."

"Hermes, as in the cat-juicers of Hermes?" There was another *click*.

"The what?" he asked. "Oh, you mean the caduceus. Yes, that's right -- the caduceus of Hermes."

Suddenly I had two connections -- *click, click* -- one after the other, just like that! The pyramid symbol on the bogus Wing

Kundalini Conspiracy Page 37

Commander's cap badge. And the caduceus, which the aforementioned Wing Commander had claimed was a pictorial representation of Kundalini energy. Thoth -- pyramids -- Kundalini.... Things were starting to fit together!

I scribbled some notes and then asked another question. "These rituals that the Servants of Thoth are supposed to perform on Dogbarrow Hill -- do you know what goes on, exactly?"

"It's a deeply religious experience," Reverend Odling said. "Involving total abnegation of the self -- total subjugation to the will of Thoth. We go into a deep trance... I mean, the cult members go into a deep trance. That's what I gather from the ones I've spoken to, I mean."

I nodded. "I see. And is there any -- um -- sexual aspect to these rituals?"

"The Servants of Thoth serve Thoth sexually, just as they serve him in every other way. They allow him to penetrate their inner being."

"The women allow him to penetrate them?" I asked. "All the women?"

"And all the men, too," he said. "He penetrates all the cult members. It's a deeply blissful experience -- or so I'm led to believe. Are you thinking of joining the cult? If you are then I think I could put you in touch with the right people."

I felt myself turning white. There are limits to what even a professional paranormal investigator can be expected to go through in the course of an investigation. I decided I'd have to find some other way of following up the leads the vicar had given me. I made my excuses and left.

Kundalini Conspiracy

9

HOODOO HOMICIDE

When I got home I found a reply to my advertisement waiting for me. It had only been a couple of days ago that I'd pinned my card onto the bulletin board at the Mystic Mall, but so much had happened in the interim that I'd almost forgotten about it. *Byron Bland, investigator of the Paranormal, the Unexplained and the generally Weird. No job too small, rates negotiable.*

I still had the airbase and vimanas and Thoth cult to worry about, but the new case took precedence. This was a paying customer, after all. So I cycled back into Blastonbury and located number 11 Middle Street. I propped my bicycle against the limestone wall and knocked on the door.

"Mrs Millet?" I said to the birdlike old lady who opened the door. "I'm Byron Bland, the paranormal investigator."

"Ah, yes, I saw your advertisement in the Mystic Mall. Do come in." She led the way into the small, over-furnished and slightly mouldy-smelling front room. "Would you like some tea? I've just made some." She disappeared into the kitchen.

I sat down on a sofa that must have seen better days, and she returned carrying the tea and biscuits. "No-one else will listen to me," she said, perching on the chair opposite me. "But it's all too much of a coincidence, really it is."

"Perhaps you'd better start at the beginning," I said, sipping my tea. I looked and sounded just like a professional investigator, I decided.

"Well, it started with my Len -- he was the first," Mrs Millet said. "He was sitting drinking his tea, right where you are now, when suddenly he had this seizure and dropped down dead. A heart attack, old Doctor Warren said, although Len didn't have a history of heart problems or anything. At first the doctor thought it might be poisoning...."

I coughed and splurted out a mouthful of tea, spilling half the remainder in my lap. "Sorry, it went down the wrong way," I croaked, fumbling in my pocket for a handkerchief.

"... it could have been digitalis poisoning, going by the symptoms, Doc Warren said. But then he had some tests done and they didn't find anything. So the death certificate says heart attack -- but I still have my doubts."

"Why?" I asked. "I mean, I assume Len was getting on in years, and...."

"Oh, he was," she said. "But it's the coincidence, you see. A couple of days later exactly the same thing happened to poor Mortimer."

"Mortimer?" I asked.

"My cat. One minute he was lapping up his milk, the next he jumps two feet in the air and lands with his paws sticking up, stiff as anything." She started sobbing. "Len's death I could handle, but I really adored that cat -- he meant the world to me."

"But if the deaths weren't natural, and they weren't simple poisoning -- what do you think they were?" I asked, getting out my notebook and pencil. I was beginning to see why she'd called in a paranormal investigator.

She dried her eyes on a tissue. "It's hoodoo, that's what it is" she said. "Bad vibrations. And I know exactly where the bad vibrations are coming from. It's that Stanley Badd at number 13, you mark my words." She pointed in the direction of the next house along the street. "He's some kind of mad scientist or inventor or something, always tinkering in that workshop he's got in his back yard."

"Sounds innocent enough to me," I said. "Why do you suspect him?"

"He was always arguing with Len -- they never got on with each other. Mind you, my Len never got on with anyone very well, but Stanley Badd next door was the worst. They almost came to blows a few weeks ago."

"I guess that's a motive," I said, scribbling in my notebook. "But what about Mortimer, the cat?"

"Now that I just can't understand," she said. "He was such a loveable creature. And very territorial. All these backyards round here, Mr Badd's lawn and his flower beds -- they were all part of Mortimer's territory."

"Ah, cat shit!" I said, with sudden understanding.

"I beg your pardon?" Mrs Millet said.

"Um, I said *I'll catch it* -- or him. Or her, or them," I extemporized wildly. "Whatever or whoever was responsible for these dreadful killings. Just leave it to me."

I left the Millet residence and went to check out number 13 next door. It was a similar stone-built cottage, set back slightly from the road. There was a narrow path leading past the house to the back yard, and I could just see the large corrugated iron workshop that Mrs Millet had mentioned. But there was no chance of getting a closer look, at least not in broad daylight. The path was overlooked by both downstairs and upstairs windows in the house. But maybe from the field at the back....

I went the long way round and located the high stone wall at the back of number 13. After much clambering I managed to struggle onto the top of the wall, but then a stone came loose under my feet and I tumbled in a heap on the other side. I landed on a pile of refuse sacks, which was fortunate for two reasons. Firstly, because it broke my fall, and secondly, because I'd been intending to search the garbage for clues anyway.

One of the bags had a tear in it, and among the chicken bones and banana skins inside I could see a screwed-up piece of paper. I retrieved it and flattened it out. It was a receipt from The Mystic Mall Health Store, clearly made out to Mr Stanley Badd.

It was for just one item: *Digitalis Purpurea 30C, 25 doses, £4.99.*

I punched the air in triumph. The case was virtually sewn up already -- and this time I'd done it all by myself, with no help from Ms Jessica Tantric Elemental Peace-Lily. She could keep all her psychic talents and her body piercings and her phallic obsession. I'd finally proved that I didn't need her. I paused, feeling sure there was something I'd missed out. And her big bottom, I thought -- her really huge bottom. She could keep that, too.

10

A RELUCTANT RECRUIT

I parked my bicycle outside the Mystic Mall and went straight into the health shop. Dumpy Val Moonblade was sitting behind the counter, dressed in a black T-shirt and long skirt. Her close-cropped hair was dyed green today.

She looked up at me. "Hi there, Byron -- how's the UFO hunt going?"

"I've got a few leads," I said. "But I'll have to tell you about them some other time. I'm working on a different case at the moment. I understand you sell digitalis in this shop."

"Yes -- that's right," Val said. "It's one of our homeopathic remedies. And you're in luck. Our part-time homeopath is in today. You'll find her upstairs in Treatment Room Two."

I walked up the narrow stairs. The door to Treatment Room Two was open when I got to the top. Inside, a short, somewhat bottom-heavy female figure was standing on some steps, arranging brown glass bottles on a high shelf. She was dressed smartly in a skirt and blouse, with metal-rimmed glasses perched on her tiny upturned nose. Her mousy brown hair was tied back in a loose bun.

"Jessica -- I never thought I'd see you again!" I said. I grinned lecherously as she stepped down onto the floor.

"Oh God," she groaned, taking a couple of steps back.

"God is right," I said. "Your very own sex-god!" I looked her up and down. "You're dressed smart but you're still naked underneath. I've seen your pubic tattoo and your clit-ring."

Jessica pulled a face. "So have I," she said. "They turn me on, but you don't. I thought I warned you to stay away from me. I've half a mind to call the police right now."

"Okay, call them," I said. "You can tell them how one of your homoerotic remedies was used in the murder of one Len Millet."

"What?" she said, looking even more horrified than when she'd first seen me.

I told her about my conversation with Mrs Millet, and showed her the receipt I'd found in Stanley Badd's garbage.

"But this wouldn't poison anyone," she said. "Where it says 30C -- that means the digitalis has been diluted a hundredfold, thirty times over. So its chemical strength has been reduced by a factor of one hundred to the power of thirty. That's an enormous number. There would be very few digitalis molecules left in the solution, if any."

"A likely story," I said. "Why would anyone want to do that?"

"Because every time the chemical strength is weakened, the homeopathic potency is increased by the same factor. Homeopathy is for curing ailments, not causing them. It works on the principle of similarity -- Like cures Like. If a patient has an illness which exhibits symptoms similar to those of digitalis poisoning, then prescribing a homeopathic form of digitalis can act to alleviate the symptoms."

"But the fact remains that Len Millet died, and the prime suspect appears to have bought digitalis from this shop," I pointed out.

Jessica looked worried. "Maybe you're right," she said. "There certainly seems to be something strange going on here. Damn! It looks like I'm going to have to help you after all. My professional reputation is at stake. Okay, I'll meet you outside Mr Badd's house at midnight tonight."

I was half way downstairs when I was struck by a sudden thought. I went back to the treatment room.

"I thought I just got rid of you," Jessica said. "What is it now?"

"Do you know anything about the Servants of Thoth?" I asked.

"Yes, it's some sort of religious cult," she said. "The vicar told me about it. I think he's secretly a member himself."

"That's what I think, too," I said. "But there's more to it than that. I've got the whole thing worked out."

"I doubt it," she said.

"Did you know that Thoth was the name of a god in ancient Egypt, in the time of the pyramids?"

"Yes," she said.

"And did you know that the Greek equivalent of Thoth was Hermes, whose symbol was that cat-juicer thing?"

"Yes," she said.

"Thoth, pyramids, cat-juicers, Kundalini, vimanas... it's all beginning to fit together, isn't it?"

"No," she said.

11

KINKY KARMA

I went back downstairs into the main health food shop. Val Moonblade was still sitting behind the counter, waiting for the next customer to come in. I was about to leave the shop when an impulse took hold of me and I went over to her.

"Look, Val," I said in a low voice. "You have people doing all kinds of mystical practices and therapies, don't you?"

"Yes, of course," she said. "Is there any particular thing you're interested in?"

"Um, I was thinking about Tantric practices," I said. "Do you do that sort of thing here?" My voice had lowered even further to a conspiratorial whisper.

"Yes, as a matter of fact we do," Val said, in an equally low voice. "Both Eric and I are fully qualified to do Tantric rituals. I'd be happy to tell you more about it some time."

I looked around at the empty shop and the far-from-bustling mall outside. "What about now?" I asked. "It seems pretty quiet."

Val perked up. "Sounds great! I was getting bored sitting here. I'll just call Eric so he can take over from me behind the counter. Then we'll go downstairs. We've got a basement room that's a bit more private."

A few minutes later I was sitting on the floor of the small basement room facing Val. We were kneeling on a thin black mattress that stretched almost from wall to wall. There were a few cushions scattered around, and what looked like Tibetan tapestries hanging on the wall. The room was dimly lit by flickering candles, and the air was laden with incense. The statue of some long-forgotten goddess stood in one corner, and a huge stone phallus in another.

"You'll know the basics of Tantric theory from Jishnu's lecture a couple of days ago," Val said. "Essentially it's all about raising Kundalini energy."

"Oh, I know all about raising Kundy-loony," I said. "I do it all the time."

"You masturbate?" asked Val. "That's very enlightened. Masturbation is the central act of the Tantric ritual. It can be performed by a man alone, or by a man on another man, or by a woman on a man."

"But not by a woman on her own," I extrapolated. "Or by a woman on another woman?"

"That's right," Val said. "In the rituals we perform I work with men, and Eric works with both men and women."

I pondered that for a moment, as a vague idea started to form in my mind. "That mousy little girl upstairs," I began slowly. "The homeopath I was just talking to..."

"Jessica Peace-Lily," Val said. "A very nice girl -- rather intense, but very nice. What about her?"

"I heard her say something about being a Tantric adept," I said. "Does that mean she's into Tantric rituals?"

Val smiled. "It's difficult to picture a serious little thing like her raising Kundalini," she said. "But you can never tell. Eric would be the one to ask -- he may well have worked with Jessica. Eric's always in great demand for that sort of thing."

I looked up. "Why's that?" I asked.

"Eric's got what it takes," Val said, proudly. "He's hung like a horse. He wasn't always that big, of course, but he's worked at it for years with a vacuum pump. In the West they say size doesn't matter, but the Tantric way is different. Bigger is always better. "

I nodded glumly, remembering Jessica's remark about the size of my penis. Suddenly I knew what I had to do.

"Look, I need to see Eric," I said. "It's a question of karma. Can you get him down here for a moment?"

"Yes, of course," Val said. "I'll go upstairs and take over at the counter. He'll be down in a few minutes."

When Eric appeared he was looking a little puzzled. He sat down and crossed his long gangly legs, waiting for me to say what was on my mind.

I began rather hesitantly. "Um, Val tells me that you've, uh, got a rather large penis."

Eric stroked his beard. "I suppose that's true. It comes from years of vacuum pumping. It's the Tantric way, you see."

"Yes, Val's already explained that much," I said. "She also said that you act out Tantric rituals with a number of partners. Both male and female. Is that right?"

"It certainly is," Eric said. "Do you want to do one now? Is that what this is all about?"

I felt my face flush. "There's a girl who works here by the name of Jessica Peace-Lily," I said, ignoring Eric's question. "Do you ever do Tantric rituals with her?"

"I certainly do," Eric said. "Once a week, regular as clockwork. She's nothing like the other women I work with. The others just use the Tantric ritual as an excuse for a quick sexual thrill. But with Jessica it's a genuinely spiritual thing -- she goes about it so seriously. She's obviously got a deep mystical obsession with the phallus."

"... And she needs one as big as yours to satisfy her," I said. I'd already worked that out. "I want to see it for myself. And I want to know exactly what Jessica does with it."

Eric unzipped his jeans and pulled out a long, flaccid, snakelike member. It was at least a foot long, with distended veins running along its length. A side-effect of the vacuum pumping, no doubt.

I stared at it with a mixture of revulsion and fascination. It was impossible to reconcile that bloated, oversized thing with mousy-haired little Jessica. "It's twice the size of mine," I said. "Wh-what does the Tantric ritual involve, exactly?"

Eric started to stroke his huge organ. "Masturbation," he said. "Manual stimulation of the phallus until the Kundalini energy spurts from the tip."

I gulped. " I want to do that," I said. "I mean, I want to do it with your dick." I'd made up my mind and there was no going back.

"That's fine," Eric said. "Be my guest. I didn't realize you were bisexual."

"I'm not," I said. "But like I told Val, it's all a matter of karma. I've got to do this for the sake of my karma."

And I did.

12

TESLA TECHNOLOGY

Jessica turned up at Stanley Badd's house at midnight, just as she'd promised. She was dressed in her familiar off-white, tight-fitting karate suit. She made for the path at the side of the house.

"Not so fast," I whispered. "There's something I want to say first. I had a long talk with Eric Moonblade this afternoon. I know all about you and him."

Jessica stared at me with her pert little nostrils. "So what? He's got a decent sized penis, unlike you." She tried to get past, but I was determined to get to the end of this first.

"I know," I hissed. "I've jerked it off, just like you."

That took her by surprise. "What? I didn't know you were gay."

"I'm not," I said. "I did it because it was the closest I could get to having sex with you."

Jessica looked at me with wide open eyes for several seconds. "You're disgusting," she said finally. From the way she said it, I had the feeling she was thinking something else entirely. But I didn't know what.

I let Jessica past, and then followed her along the path to the corrugated iron workshop. It felt a lot safer doing that under the cover of darkness than it would have been during the daytime.

The door to the workshop was fastened securely with a heavy padlock. "Damn," I said. "How are we going to get in?"

"Shut up -- I need to concentrate," Jessica said, holding the padlock gently in her right hand and fixing her gaze on it.

I shut up. Jessica concentrated. After a few seconds, the padlock sprung open.

"I've been practising my psychokinesis," Jessica explained. "I never know when I'm going to need it."

We went into the workshop and switched on the light. The place was full of junk. There were several partly dismantled microwave ovens and TV sets lying around, and a jumble of wires and cables. One end of the workshop was taken up by a metal framework in the shape of a pyramid. It looked a bit like a small tent frame without any fabric. Opposite the pyramid was a fair-sized workbench.

The workbench was dominated by a large coil, surrounded by other bits and pieces including a computer, an oscilloscope, several boxes covered in knobs and dials, and other paraphernalia. A few brown glass bottles were scattered about.

"Hmm, I wonder what all this is?" Jessica said, studying the apparatus intently.

"Oh, just some electronic gizmo," I said, showing off my superior technical knowledge. Women may be all right when it comes to things like psychokinesis, but they're no good at science.

"Let's see -- there's a Tesla coil, a high-frequency signal generator, cascaded magnetrons, and a couple of microwave horns. It must be some kind of rudimentary Zero-Point projector," Jessica said thoughtfully.

"Oh, well, yes -- of course. That's so obvious it goes without saying." I began to wish I'd learnt to smoke a pipe. I bet she couldn't do that.

"The microwave horns are pointing out through the window," Jessica continued. "The beams converge on the house next door. This must be how he did it, though I can't see where the homeopathy element fits in."

There was a sudden sound behind us, and we turned to see a tall lugubrious figure standing in the doorway. He was dressed in pajamas and a bathrobe, and had what appeared to be a large saucepan on his head. He was pointing a double-barreled shotgun at us.

"Stanley Badd?" I presumed.

"The very same," he said. "And I compliment your partner on her shrewd assessment of my little constructional project."

"His *professional* partner," Jessica corrected hastily, putting what I felt was an unnecessarily strong emphasis on the word professional. "But what you're doing here is a dreadful perversion, using my homeopathic remedies to murder the innocent."

"Innocent, my foot!" Stanley said. "No-one will miss either the man or the cat. I was doing the world a service by getting rid of them. I'm quite a heroic figure, really. You've got to consider the bigger picture. For more than fifty years, Zero-Point technology has been under the exclusive control of the government -- the secret weapon by which they've kept ordinary people in check. They get inside our minds and make us do things against our will.... Unless we take precautions, of course." He tapped the saucepan on his head. "It's a Faraday shield, you see. It keeps the bad vibrations out. And now that I've discovered the secret of Zero-Point for myself, I'm starting to get my own back."

Stanley went over to the workbench and sat by the computer console, still pointing the shotgun at us. "It's all a matter of modulation," he continued. "To provoke a physical effect on the body, the Zero-Point field needs to be modulated with an appropriate chemical signature. This is where your homeopathic remedies come in. Although the chemical is no longer present, its vibrational signature remains in the solution indefinitely. That's how homeopathy works, and how I was able to project its effects via electromagnetic waves into the house next door."

Stanley switched on the computer and started typing with his left hand, all the time keeping us covered with the gun. "To get more subtle mind-control effects, it's necessary to use computer-generated digital modulations. You can make people do anything you want -- buy things they don't need, vote for people they don't like, watch mindless drivel on the TV...."

I suddenly had an idea. "Can you fill someone with the desire to have sex with another person?" I asked. "A specific other person, I mean?"

"It's the easiest thing in the world," Stanley said. "That was the first program I ever wrote. Deep down, everyone wants to have sex with everyone else. It's just a question of breaking down a person's better judgment. In another sense, that's what the government's been doing to us for years. For a long time, they were limited to projecting their mind-control programs from a distance, which dilutes their effect dramatically. What they really needed was some way of persuading their victims to hold a microwave source right up against their skulls. For decades they struggled with the problem -- after all, even the ignorant masses weren't *that* stupid. Then finally they invented cellphones, and all over the world people have played right into their hands."

"Cellphones are a capitalist plot to make money out of the weak-minded and gullible, through advertizing hype and ruthless marketeering," Jessica said.

"I've got a cellphone," I said, proudly tapping the handset on my belt.

"That proves my point," said Jessica.

"And mine," said Stanley. He lapsed into silence, as he continued his one-handed typing for several minutes.

"Are you going to kill us, too?" I asked.

"Oh, good heavens, no," Stanley said. "You haven't done me any harm. Not like that old bugger next door and his damn cat. No, I'm just going to play around with your minds a bit, to make sure you no longer pose a threat to me."

"You'll never get away with this, Stanley," I said. "You ought to know that my glamorous assistant here is a Black Belt in karate and all sorts of other lethal stuff. She's going to make mincemeat out of you the moment you drop your guard."

"I doubt it," Stanley said. "Take a look at her."

I glanced at Jessica, who looked back at me with a blissfully dumb expression. She stuck out her tongue and giggled.

"What have you done to her?" I asked, horrified.

"I'm just irradiating the room with a standard government-issue dumbing-down program," Stanley said. "It drastically reduces attention span, discrimination and other higher brain functions."

"But why is it only affecting her, not me?"

"Your friend is obviously a very smart young lady. I've found that susceptibility to this program is proportional to IQ. The more intelligent the subject, the faster the program takes effect. Never mind... it'll catch up with you eventually. I'll let it go to work on the two of you for the rest of the night. By morning it should be safe for me to release you."

Stanley found several pieces of rope, and tied our wrists and ankles. Then he crawled inside the framework pyramid and crossed his legs. There was a wire hanging down from the frame, which he clipped onto the saucepan thing on his head. What had he called it? His Faraday shield. I wasn't sure what happened when you connected a Faraday shielded saucepan to a metal pyramid, but Stanley seemed to go into some sort of trance. Anyway, his eyes were closed and he no longer seemed to be paying any attention to us.

It all depended on me now, I realized. There was very little time in which to act. It was probably only a matter of minutes before Stanley's dumbing-down program would take its inexorable effect on me. I started to think frantically.

13

PYRAMID POWER

I was still thinking frantically several hours later when the sun came up. For some reason the dumbing-down program wasn't working on me. From what Stanley had said, that either meant that I had an extremely low IQ, or.... Well, I couldn't think what else it might have meant, but I was sure there was a logical explanation of some kind. Whatever it was, it had given me plenty of time to think. But even after racking my brains all night, I hadn't thought up a way to get us out of there. Stanley had left me with my cellphone, but I couldn't get to it because my hands were tied behind my back. If Jessica had been her normal self she could have loosened the ropes with her psychokinesis, but as it was she just sat there with a foolish grin on her face, humming inanely.

As daylight grew, Stanley slowly seemed to come out of his trance. He opened his eyes, unclipped the wire from the saucepan, and clambered out of the pyramid. Now, you can say what you like about my IQ, but at least I was intelligent enough to pretend the program had worked. I adopted the same blissfully dumb expression as Jessica.

Stanley untied me, and then moved over to Jessica. As soon as his back was turned, I whipped the saucepan off his head and hit him with it as hard as I could. He fell onto his knees, dazed. I tied him up with the ropes he'd taken off me, and then finished untying Jessica. Now came the tricky part -- how was I going to get her back to normal?

I went over to Stanley's computer and looked at the screen. The cursor was flashing against a button labeled "*Dumbing down*". Next to it there was another button labeled "*Undo*". I moved the cursor onto it, but then I suddenly remembered something Stanley had said earlier. I scrolled up to the top of the menu. Sure enough, the first button was labeled "*SEX*". I grinned and placed the cursor over it. But then I hesitated -- why interfere with the natural course of things? After all, I could sense that Jessica was beginning to fall in love with me, even without electronic assistance. I moved the cursor back down the menu and clicked on the button to undo the dumbing-down program.

A few minutes later Jessica blinked and glared at me. "About time too, dickhead," she said.

My jaw dropped. "What do you mean?"

"Just because my higher brain functions were scrambled doesn't mean I wasn't aware what was going on," she said. "It's simply that I was powerless to do anything about it. And so were you, for that matter, although Stanley's Zero-Point machine didn't have anything to do with that."

"Isn't Zero-Point the same thing as Kundy-loony?" I asked. "That's what Jishnu Mitra said in his lecture. I think Adastra said it as well."

"That's right," Jessica said, looking thoughtful. "Zero-Point energy and Kundalini energy are aspects of the same thing. There's a connection here, if only I could see it." She wandered over to inspect Stanley's pyramid. "Pyramids, pyramids, pyramids.... First there was the pyramid on Adastra's cap badge, and now this. It's got something to do with mind control, I think. Stanley thought he was controlling people's minds with his machine, but maybe someone else was controlling him with the pyramid."

"Someone else or some*thing* else," I said, in the knee-jerk response of a seasoned paranormal investigator.

"... Or some*thing* else," Jessica echoed. "He certainly seemed to be in a trance of some kind. There's more to this than meets the eye."

She wandered back to the workbench and looked at the computer screen. "Now, what are we going to do with Mr Badd here?" She took the mouse from me and scrolled up and down the list. "Ah, this looks just the thing." She clicked on a button labeled "*Tell the truth, the whole truth, and nothing but the truth*".

"I was just about to suggest that myself," I said, getting the words out quickly before the truth program started to take effect. "What do we do now?"

"Now we make an anonymous call to the police. By the time they get here we'll be gone, and Stanley will be ready to make a full confession."

"Good thinking," I said. "Would you like to borrow my cellphone?"

"Uh, no thanks," Jessica said, wrinkling her nose.

"Why not?" I asked. "Because cellphones are a capitalist plot to make money out of gullible people, or because they're a government mind-control device?"

"Because it's your phone, and I'd probably catch some dreadful contagious disease off it."

Kundalini Conspiracy

14

THOUSANDS OF THEORIES

I spent the next couple of days doing some serious background research. I was determined to get to the bottom of the weird things that had been going on, and felt that some sort of pattern was finally starting to emerge. It was something to do with pyramids, and something to do with mind control. Okay, so maybe Jessica had said that first, but I would have got there eventually. As for the rest of it.... Well, I was going to work the rest out for myself. Jessica had made it clear that I wouldn't get any more help from her. But that was fine -- I didn't need her help. Byron Bland wasn't the sort of paranormal investigator who needed a junior sidekick tagging along.

It was a bit like putting a jigsaw together. I had some of the pieces, and it was just a matter of working out how they fit together. A methodical approach was called for. I started to review the evidence I had so far.

The pyramid symbol had first turned up on the cap badge of that Adastra guy, who said he was an Air Force officer but probably wasn't. Not regular Air Force, anyhow. The phoney Air Force people were back-engineering ancient technology from a long lost Indian civilization -- a civilization that had existed way back when Atlantis was still around. They had a flying machine called a vimana, which worked on Kundalini energy and looked just like a UFO. The phoney Air Force people flew around in it pretending to be aliens.

Which brought me to my first theory. What if the phoney aliens were real aliens? In other words, aliens posing as people posing as aliens? That would certainly have made a lot of sense. Not all aliens had gray skins and big eyes. Some of them were shape-shifters who could pose as human beings within arousing suspicion. The more I thought about it, the more likely it sounded.

But how did that fit in with Stanley Badd and his mind control equipment? Stanley thought he was beating the government at their own game, but when he sat inside the pyramid thing it was as if some other force took hold of him. Could that have been the aliens as well? Or was it the government? Was Stanley doing the government's sinister bidding without even realizing it?

And what about the mysterious cult, the Servants of Thoth? Where did they fit in, if at all? The shadowy figure who called himself Thoth -- was he one of the aliens, or was he working for the government? Were the phoney airmen members of the cult? And Stanley Badd -- was he a servant of Thoth, too?

Perhaps I needed to take a different approach. Pyramids came from ancient Egypt, as did the name Thoth. Vimanas came from ancient India. Maybe the link was in the past, not the present. I thought of Erich von Daniken and all the evidence he'd brought to light concerning ancient astronauts -- visitors from space that were recorded in the Bible and other religious texts. Then there was Immanuel Velikovsky, who had shown that ancient myths of floods and catastrophes weren't myths at all, but records of real events.

I felt I was onto something. The jigsaw was starting to look like a meaningful picture. What I needed now was more information about ancient civilizations -- a lot more. I got on my bicycle and rode into Blastonbury.

I borrowed a stack of books from the public library, loading my rucksack with the works of Charles Fort, Graham Hancock and others of that ilk. Then I popped into the Mystic Mall's psychic bookstore and splashed out on a few second-hand paperbacks. That should be enough to keep me going for a while, I thought. After all, there was the internet to scour, as well.

I was on the point of returning home when I was struck by a sudden thought. I made my way to the sleazier side of town and went into one of the grimy little shops there. When I came out I was the proud owner of the latest model top-of-the-range electronic vacuum pump.

I rode home quickly, keen to get back to my research. And to try out the vacuum pump. But not necessarily in that order.

As it turned out, I could do both things at the same time. Once I'd slipped the vacuum pump over my penis and switched it on, the rest was automatic. I zipped up my jeans and sat down to do some serious reading. The gadget made an impressive bulge in my crotch, but if it worked as advertized I'd be making just as big a bulge even without the vacuum pump. In no time at all, my organ would be as big as Eric Moonblade's. I was going to be a Tantric sex-god! If Jessica was lucky, I might let her have some of my Kundalini energy. If she wasn't lucky (and she might not be), then I'd keep it all to myself.

I began my research by reading up on the ancient Egyptian gods, starting with the likes of Thoth and Osiris. Then I took a look at some of the lesser known ones, and almost immediately came up with another piece that fitted the jigsaw. One of the older Egyptian deities was called Nyarlathotep, who was mentioned in the dread *Necronomicon* of Abdul Alhazred. In that hideous old tome Nyarlathotep was referred to as the "crawling chaos" and the "all-seeing eye". The latter phrase immediately made me think of the eye inside the pyramid on the phoney Air Force badge. There was even a hint that Thoth and Nyarlathotep were different aspects of the same entity. Pyramids -- Egypt -- Thoth -- Nyarlathotep -- the all-seeing eye.... I was sure I was onto something now!

The next step was to link it all to Kundalini and the Rama Empire. And I knew exactly who could help me out on that score. After all, I knew an expert in the field -- Jishnu Mitra, the man who'd given the public lecture last week. I picked up my cellphone and called the Mystic Mall. To my relief, it was Val

Moonblade who answered, rather than Eric. I was a little shy about speaking to Eric after our last encounter.

"Hello, Val," I said. "It's Byron here, your favorite paranormal investigator and Tantric initiate. I'm working on another case. Can you give me a number for Jishnu Mitra, please?"

Val did so, and I tapped in the digits. The phone rang for a few moments, then Jishnu answered.

"Hi, Jishnu," I said. "You don't know me, but my name's Byron Bland. I'm a paranormal investigator and I was in the audience for your lecture last week. That's right, the one at the Mystic Mall. I've got a couple of questions for you, if you don't mind. First of all, do you know if they had pyramids in ancient India -- I mean pyramids like the ones in Egypt? And does the name Nyarlathotep means anything to you?"

Jishnu gave me a rather long answer, but what it boiled down to was "No" and "No", respectively. We went on to have a more general chat about my investigation, and he offered to help me out any time I needed more information on ancient India. In the meantime, he suggested that perhaps I ought to have a closer look at the works of Richard Shaver concerning Lemuria. I thanked him and rang off.

I was vaguely aware that Lemuria was some kind of lost continent that had flourished around the same time as Atlantis. I'd also heard of Richard Shaver, who had written about a previous life he'd lived as a citizen of Lemuria. But at Jishnu's suggestion I dug out an old book called *The Shaver Mystery*, and read it from cover to cover.

Another piece of the jigsaw fell into place! Shaver's work told of an Elder Race that had inhabited the surface of the Earth before humans had appeared. The Elder Race had never completely died out, but lived on to this day in huge caverns deep within the planet. They had advanced technology that sounded like vimanas and UFOs, and mind control devices that they used on unsuspecting humans. I was getting close to the answer, I felt sure. Perhaps Nyarlathotep himself was a member of Shaver's Elder Race!

Over time, according to Shaver, parts of the Elder Race had regressed to a degenerate form. In particular, Shaver's world was home to every imaginable form of sexual debauchery. There were submissive females with furry tails like cats, and dominant females with forty-foot high bodies and six arms. I paid particularly close attention to these chapters, unzipping my jeans as I read.

With a jolt of surprise, I realized I was still wearing the vacuum pump. I switched it off and removed it. My penis showed no obvious signs of growth, but it was early days yet. I took it in my hand and went back to work, reading all about the Shaver mystery. Sexual debauchery, gigantic women, girls with furry tails.... Pure bliss!

15

STANDING STONES

It was a week to the day since it had all started. A week since I'd pinned my business card to the Mystic Mall's bulletin board. A week since I'd attended Jishnu's lecture. A week since I'd been abducted by the phoney Air Force officers in their back-engineered vimana. A week since I'd met Jessica Peace-Lily for the first time.

I was looking forward to the evening, when Nik Shaman would be at the Mystic Mall to give his much-heralded lecture on *Chaos Theory and Sacred Resonance*. But that was still several hours away. The day started when I came downstairs and found the local newspaper waiting for me on the doormat.

I read the paper from cover to cover, following as ever in the footsteps of Charles Fort. It was a good thing I did. Right there in black and white at the bottom of page seven was another piece of the jigsaw. "*Cattle mutilations continue*", the headline read. From what little information the report contained, I gathered that cows in one of the local fields were being mutilated and killed on a regular basis -- one cow every two or three nights. The cause of death was unknown, but the symptoms were always the same. The carcasses had been drained of blood, and the sex organs cored out with surgical precision. The newspaper put the blame on a large lynx or puma, but I knew better than that.

The report had all the hallmarks of a classic animal mutilation case. I knew right away that it had nothing at all to do with lynxes or pumas. Cases of this kind are commoner in the United States than they are here, but they've been reported all over the world. They're often associated with crop circles, and almost invariably with UFO activity. And right here, right now, UFOs meant back-engineered vimanas. This was another case for Byron Bland, paranormal investigator!

I cycled out to the field where the mutilations had occurred. It lay in the lee of Dogbarrow Hill, near the site of my abduction experience the week before. I scoured the field inch by inch, but I was unable to detect any of the tell-tale signs that would have revealed a recent UFO landing spot. At one corner of the field there was a derelict barn, now empty and largely open to the elements. Beyond that was an extensive wheat field, but all the stalks were boringly upright -- not a hint of a crop circle or saucer landing nest.

I started to walk back to my bike when I spotted something on the ground that I'd missed the first time. I bent down to pick it up. It was a sparkling red crystal, like something I might have carried in my toolbox in my previous life as a Vimana mechanic back in ancient India. It would have fitted perfectly into the ship's crystal yantra, though I had no idea what effect it would have produced. Its shape wasn't quite like any of the crystals I remembered....

Then it hit me. The shape of the crystal I was holding... it was a perfect pyramid! It was about an inch on a side, and identical in shape to the pyramids I'd seen in Stanley Badd's workshop and on Wing Commander Adastra's cap badge! "Pyramids, pyramids, pyramids", Jessica had said. Well, now I was one pyramid ahead of her!

As I walked slowly back to the edge of the field, I thought I caught a glimpse of movement amongst the prehistoric stones on top of Dogbarrow Hill. I stopped and got out my binoculars for a better look. I could hardly believe my eyes. "*Speak of the devil, and she'll appear.*" It was a diminutive, mousy-haired figure in a yellowing, tight-fitting martial arts outfit! She seemed to be doing something very unnatural with the stones. What on Earth was she up to?

I returned the binoculars to their case, and hurried over to the footpath leading up the hill. I started to climb towards the stone circle. Everyone had heard of Stonehenge, but most people thought it was a one-off. Well, in terms of size and complexity that was true -- Stonehenge was unique. But there were hundreds of smaller stone circles all over the British Isles. The one on top of Dogbarrow Hill was one of the less impressive specimens. Just half a dozen small stones, not much taller than a person. Adjacent to the stones was an elongated mound of earth with a rough stone facing. This was a prehistoric burial chamber -- a long-barrow. It was what gave Dogbarrow Hill its name.

Jessica saw me coming as I approached. "Oh, no -- not you again," she said. "It was so peaceful up here."

"What were you doing?" I asked. "It looked like you were trying to have sex with one of the stones."

"The stones represent the sacred Lingam," she said. "The male organ... of which you have a particularly pathetic example, if I remember correctly. I use the stones to recharge my elemental energies. I told you before -- I'm the Earth element. Copulating with the stones brings me into direct communion with the Earth."

I looked at her for a minute, but she didn't blink. "What about the mystery of the vimanas and pyramids and all that?" I asked, trying to sound as if I wasn't overly concerned about it. "Are you getting any closer to solving it?"

"Oh, yes," she said. "A lot closer. How about you?"

"Oh, I'm very close," I said. We looked at each other. I wasn't going to tell her about the little crystal pyramid if she didn't give me anything in return. She didn't give me anything.

"It's too crowded up here," Jessica said. She started to walk away.

I called after her. "I suppose you'll be at Nik Shaman's lecture this evening."

She turned briefly. "I wouldn't miss it for anything," she said, then carried on down the hill.

"I'll see you there, then," I said. She didn't answer.

Kundalini Conspiracy

After Jessica had gone, I spent a few minutes wandering around the standing stones. Then I went over to look at the long-barrow. The facing stones that were visible from a distance formed an entrance-way into the chamber, which was lined internally with more stones of the same kind. I crawled inside. After about ten feet, the way was blocked by a big flat stone. It was almost like a door, but with no handle or any other way of opening it.

In the dim light filtering in from outside, I could make out some crudely lettered inscriptions on the stone, seemingly of more recent date than the burial chamber itself. One particularly intriguing inscription announced that "*Claire Voyant will suck dicks 4 cash.*" Below this there was a phone number, which I carefully noted down in the back of my diary.

Then I crawled out of the long-barrow, dusted off my jeans, and headed back down to where I'd left my bike. There was nothing else I could do here until after dark -- that would be when the cattle mutilators would strike. And when they did, I'd be down in the field waiting for them.

16

ORAL ORACLE

As soon as I got home, I phoned the number I'd written down in my diary. A female voice answered.

"Hello, is that Claire?" I asked.

"That's right, Claire Voyant," she said, in a high-pitched sing-song voice. "How can I help you?"

"Well, I... uh, I saw your advertisement," I mumbled, not quite sure how to phrase it. "I was wondering exactly what sort of service it is that you offer."

"I'm a Tarot reader," she said. "Isn't that what it says in the advertisement?"

"Yes, yes, of course," I said. "A Tarot reader. I just wanted to make sure."

"Well, are you going to make an appointment or aren't you?" she asked.

"Sure, why not?" I said. After all, I thought -- it might even help me out with the case I'm working on. A paranormal investigator shouldn't turn his nose up at any source of information, especially a mystical one. I made an appointment for later that day.

The time for the appointment came round, and I went to the address she'd given me on the phone. Claire Voyant -- if that was her real name, which I doubted very much -- answered the door when I rang the bell. She was a short, thin girl, probably in her mid-twenties but looking younger. She had long blonde hair, and was dressed in a pink leotard and red tights. At first glance, she seemed attractive enough. Then she gave me a big grin, and I saw that her front teeth had all been filed down to sharp points. Her fingernails looked pretty lethal too -- they were at least two inches long and as sharply pointed as her teeth. I wasn't sure if the nails were natural or not. They were painted blue, to match her lipstick.

Claire led me inside and sat me down at the consulting table. She remained standing at my side.

"So, you want a Tarot reading?" she said. "Is that all?"

"Uh, I think so," I said. "What else do you do?"

"Nothing," she said. "I'm just a Tarot reader. But I'm a very good one. I've got psychic powers."

I shifted uncomfortably. It was becoming obvious that Claire Voyant wasn't what you'd call a bright girl.

Claire spread her legs slightly and put her long-nailed hands to her crotch. She looked at me to make sure I was watching. "This is where my power comes from," she said. She pulled up the crotch of the leotard until it was so tight it revealed every contour of her anatomy. "Looks good, doesn't it?" she asked. She stroked herself lasciviously a few times. "Mmm... feels good too. That's got me all juiced up and ready to go. Now we can do the reading."

Claire took the seat opposite me. She picked up the deck of cards that had been sitting in the middle of the table and started to shuffle it.

"Is there any particular question that you want answering?" she asked.

By this time I'd lost all hope that she'd be any help to me, but I made an effort anyway. "I'm a paranormal investigator," I said. "I'm working on a particularly difficult case at the moment."

"Ooh, how interesting!" Claire said. "I'm sure I'll be able to help you. I'm very talented, you know."

She dealt out five cards face down -- one in the center, then four others above, below and to left and right of the first.

The first card tells me about your present situation," she said, turning over the top card. "The Emperor -- how interesting! The emperor is a phallic symbol, you know. That means a man's penis. This card represents your penis."

I watched as she turned over the cards to the left and right of the first.

"These two cards represent waning influences and emerging influences," she said. "Ooh, look -- the Ace of Wands and the Ten of Wands. The Wand is a phallic symbol, of course. The Ace means a little penis, and the Ten means a lot of little penises, or one big one. Have you got a big penis, Mr Bland?"

"It's getting bigger day by day," I mumbled, wishing we could get to the end of this a bit more quickly.

Claire clapped her hands. "There you are, then!" she said, flashing her sharply pointed teeth. "It's getting bigger! The little penis waning and the big penis emerging. It's all working just as it's supposed to, you see. The cards are always right."

Finally, she turned over the last two cards -- the one at the bottom and the one in the center. They were the King of Swords and the Tower, respectively. Even without psychic powers, I knew what was coming next.

"Oh my goodness, two more phallic symbols!" she announced. "The hidden influence at the bottom, and the synthesis in the center. So we've got five cards, and they're all phallic symbols! I bet you've got a really nice penis, Mr Bland."

"Not everyone thinks so," I said, thinking ruefully of Jessica.

"Oh, I'm sure it's a very nice penis," Claire said. "A very, very nice penis. I love penises -- I like to suck them. In fact I'll do just that for a little extra payment. I bet you didn't know that, did you?"

"No, I didn't," I lied. I couldn't be bothered to mention the graffiti up on Dogbarrow Hill.

"Not many people do," she said. "It's my secret. But I do it with a lot of clients. I use my teeth --" she grinned broadly, showing the viciously pointed fangs, "-- and my nails as well." She held up a long-nailed finger and licked it slowly along its length. Then she slipped it in her mouth and started to fellate it.

I'd had more enticing offers, but sex was sex after all. "I'm afraid I haven't got much money with me," I said. "How much extra payment, exactly?"

She named her figure. With considerable relief and only a little disappointment, I realized it was more than I could afford. It was certainly a lot more than the little slapper was worth.

I paid her for the reading, then made a hasty exit. Looking at my watch, I realized there were only a few minutes to go before Nik Shaman's lecture was due to start. I had to get over to the Mystic Mall quickly.

17

THE GOTHIC GURU

When I got to the meeting room it was already filling up with people. Nik Shaman always drew the crowds -- in New Age circles he was a major celebrity. His books were best-sellers, and he was a familiar face on TV. Everyone wanted to hear him talk about *Chaos Theory and Sacred Resonance*.

As I mingled with the throng, I caught sight of Eric Moonblade at the front of the hall. I waved at him rather sheepishly, and he waved back. Then I spotted Nik Shaman. He was busy setting up a projector, surrounded by a group of mainly female admirers. Shaman was an imposing sight -- well over six feet tall, and dressed in a dark, double-breasted suit worn over a black T-shirt. He had shoulder-length black hair and was radiating charisma like a slick gothic Guru.

In contrast to Shaman, the bulk of the audience seemed to be made up of indistinguishable nobodies. About fifty plastic chairs had been set out in ragged lines, which were rapidly filling up as people milled into the hall. The men all seemed to be middle-aged and unshaven, with empty faces, shabby brown raincoats, and worn-out plastic shopping bags. The women were largely middle-aged and overweight, with long hair, long skirts, rings on all their fingers and jeweled studs in their noses.

Not everyone was middle-aged, though. I spotted the person I was looking for and made a bee-line for that familiar little figure in the tight-fitting, off-white martial arts suit. There was an empty seat next to her.

"Mind if I sit here?" I asked.

"No, I suppose not," she said dreamily. There was the trace of a smile on her face.

"You're in a good mood," I said. "What's the occasion?"

Jessica looked at me. "I think I'm in love," she said. Her eyes were big enough to fall into.

"I knew it would happen eventually," I said. I sniffed my armpit. "It must have been the deodorant that finally clinched it."

"Not in love with you, dickhead," Jessica said. "In love with *him*." She indicated Nik Shaman. "Isn't he gorgeous? He can have his way with me any day of the week." She gazed reverently at the figure in black at the front of the hall. "He's tall, strong and rugged -- and so intelligent! Everything a smart young Tantric Elemental could want."

I snorted in disgust. "How come women never go all gooey over short, skinny guys with pimples and glasses?" I asked.

"Well, I think I probably would," she said. "If I ever met one with brains and a personality, that is."

"I think I'm going to kill myself," I decided.

"Do you want flowers?" Jessica asked.

"What?" I said.

"At your funeral. You said you were going to kill yourself. Would you like me to send flowers?" Jessica repeated.

"Oh God. My stomach hurts," I groaned.

"Shut up," Jessica said. "He's about to start."

Shaman began his lecture with a series of slides showing prehistoric sites from around the world. Then he started to describe the Sacred Resonance theory that he'd expounded so many times before. According to Shaman, the builders of the stone circles and other monuments had placed them -- either consciously or unconsciously -- at resonant nodes of the Earth's vibrational structure. In this way, the sacred energies could be channeled for the greater good of the people.

The lights had been lowered when Shaman started talking. In the darkness I leaned back, stretched my arm out behind Jessica's chair, and toyed with the idea of putting it round her shoulder. But just as the thought started to form in my mind, there was a blur of motion in front of me and a sharp pain in my groin. It was uncanny -- it was almost as if I'd been punched firmly in the genitals. I decided to keep my hands in my lap for the rest of the lecture.

Nik Shaman went on to talk about Chaos Theory. This part of the lecture was pretty heavy on mathematics, and I didn't follow all of it. But finally he got around to explaining how Chaos Theory and Sacred Resonance fitted together. The problem lay in modern technology like TV and satellites, Shaman said. These interfered with the sacred Earth vibrations and caused them to become chaotic. As a result, the sacred sites became a nexus of evil instead of good.

An idea started nagging at me. I was sure there was something in all this that related to the case I was working on. Sacred energies, ancient sites, a nexus of evil.... There was definitely a connection, but I couldn't quite put my finger on it.

The lecture finished and there was a prolonged round of applause. Then we stood up to leave.

Jessica turned to me. "Right, so now you're off to kill yourself, are you?" she asked. "I'd like to say I'll miss you, but I'm sure I won't."

"Nope, I've changed my mind," I said. "Women aren't worth it. Anyway, I'm working on an important case -- cattle mutilations in the field by Dogbarrow Hill. Duty calls."

"Make sure you keep away from the standing stones," Jessica warned. "It's the full moon tonight, and I need to recharge my Tantric energies. I'd really hate it if you got in the way."

"Don't worry, I'll be down in the field," I said. After a pause I added "Witch" (but not out loud).

18

NIGHT-TIME NECROMANCY

Under the cover of darkness, I concealed myself in the ramshackle barn in the corner of the field. I was ready for a long vigil. The cattle were settling down for the night, the silence broken only by an increasingly infrequent moo.

As the full moon rose in the sky, I could see a diminutive figure in a white costume moving about on top of Dogbarrow Hill. Obviously it was Jessica and her stupid ritual -- shagging the Earth or whatever the hell it was she was doing. "Frankly, my dear, I don't give a damn," I thought up at her. I'd got real work to do.

For a long time, nothing happened in the field. When the action did start, it was sudden and dramatic.

First, the vimana materialized, hovering over the field. Obviously it had been cloaked with the Maya crystal, or whatever it was called. Then the vimana shot out a massive bolt of Kundalini energy, which was so intense it looked almost solid. It swooped and soared over the field -- a seething, glowing mass of pure Tantric energy. It had a distinctly phallic shape. It zoomed towards one of the terrified cows and rammed into its rear end. A second later a fountain of blood shot out of the cow's mouth.

The cow fell lifeless to the ground, its blood drained and its sex organs cored out. I'd witnessed a classic mutilation phenomenon at first hand!

The Kundalini energy was blending with the blood from the cow into something powerful, malignant and distinctly not of this earth. It reared up in a great pillar of crimson light, a huge throbbing phallus of evil. Slowly it shrank back to the ground, darkening and solidifying. It started moving diagonally across the field, taking increasingly coherent form as it went. With sudden horror, I realized it had transformed itself into human shape. And with greater horror, as the figure passed yards from my hiding place, I saw that it was none other than Nik Shaman! Jessica's oh-so-handsome idol wasn't even human... he was some kind of cow-mutilating alien, or shape-shifting demon or something!

The Shaman-thing continued purposefully on its way. I realized with a sinking heart that it was headed towards Dogbarrow Hill and the ancient stone circle. But Jessica was up there! I had to do something. I followed as closely as I dared, keeping out of sight in the shadows.

By the time I got to the top of the hill, there was no sign of either Jessica or Shaman. I looked around wildly. The landscape was clear enough in the moonlight, but they were nowhere to be seen. I went over to the long-barrow and peered inside. It was too dark to see anything. I took off my rucksack and fumbled inside for my flashlight. With the aid of its dim light I saw that the stone "door" at the back of the burial chamber had been pushed aside. Beyond it, a steep flight of steps led downwards into the depths of the earth. There was nothing else for it. I started to clamber down the stone staircase.

The ancient steps went deep into the bowels of the earth. I thought of Richard Shaver and his Elder Race, dwelling in their huge subterranean caves. Maybe that was the answer -- maybe Shaman was a survivor of the Elder Race. My mind went back to the book I'd read the other day. The Elder Race was supposed to have wondrous flying machines and high technology, so it all fitted in. Obviously I was on the way down to one of their ancient caverns. Perhaps I'd meet a giant six-armed dominatrix, or a submissive little female with a cat-like tail. I started to feel more upbeat about it all. Things got pretty racy down in those caverns, if Shaver was to be believed. The Elder Race was kinkier than kinky!

At the bottom of the steps, I found a narrow tunnel hewn into the solid rock. I shone my flashlight into it. The tunnel appeared to descend gently to yet further depths. I shrugged and set off along it.

As I made my way along the meandering tunnel, I became aware of a faint sound. It was a strange, distant rhythm -- almost like monastic chanting. I continued along the tunnel, and the chanting steadily grew louder. I was approaching its source. Based on what I'd learned from Shaver's book, it was probably some kind of seedy sado-masochistic orgy. I was going to have to get in there and mingle with the crowd. I'd probably have to shag a few furry cat-women before I got around to rescuing Jessica.

I rounded a bend in the tunnel, and just beyond I saw that it opened out into a huge rocky cavern. Exactly as I'd been expecting! I switched off my flashlight and approached the mouth of the cave. Surprisingly, there was a dim light emanating from inside. The cavern seemed to be lit by a kind of phosphorescence that came from the rocks themselves. Just inside the mouth of the cave was a massive boulder, which obscured the greater part of the cavern from my view. Yet the chanting was so clear now I was sure its source lay only yards away. I crept up to the boulder and crouched behind it, wondering what to do next.

19

A RAUNCHY RITUAL

Squatting in the shadow of the great boulder, I listened to the rhythmic chanting. It was in a language I'd never heard before. Strange, meaningless syllables were repeated over and over again... "*Sph'nagh ekk-ankh fl'hurr Azathoth....*"

Azathoth! The name rang bells in my mind. Surely Azathoth was some dire myth -- something out of the *Necronomicon*, that ancient book of dreadful wisdom penned by mad old Abdul Alhazred. The earliest editions of that notorious tome had been hand-written in blood, and bound in covers made from human flesh. I'd bought my own copy of the *Necronomicon* a few days ago, from the second-hand bookshop in the Mystic Mall. My copy wasn't one of the ones written in blood and bound in flesh, though -- just a battered old mass-market paperback from the 1970s.

I wracked my brains. Azathoth.... What was it the author of the *Necronomicon* had whispered insanely half-way through Chapter 3? Something about "... the blind idiot god Azathoth, an amorphous blight of nethermost confusion which blasphemes and bubbles at the center of all infinity." Yes, that was it. Azathoth was the primal chaos, and not a pleasant customer by any account. But surely that was just a myth? Something that was intended symbolically, rather than literally? I certainly hoped so.

I decided to risk a closer look. The Azathoth chant was probably something the Elder Race did before an orgy to get themselves going. I crept around the side of the boulder until I could get a clearer view towards the center of the cavern. When I did, my heart sank.

There was no sizzling orgy, and no six-armed giantesses or furry-tailed cat-girls. There was just a small group of figures clustered around a stone pyramid. There were about twenty of them, clad in monastic-style robes. They continued to chant, oblivious to my presence. I recognized some of them. There were Adastra and Scimitar, and some of the other phoney airmen. And Stanley Badd was there too, and Reverend Odling. Obviously these were the Servants of Thoth. They appeared to be in some kind of trance state, just as Odling had said. They looked like zombies that were being controlled by someone else.

I had a shrewd idea who that someone else was. Standing arrogantly to one side, arms folded in front of him, was the dark-robed figure of Nik Shaman. He was at least a head taller than any of the others. The focus of his gaze was on the pyramid -- on a side of the pyramid that I couldn't see from my present vantage point.

I started to edge my way round the wall of the cavern, to get a better view of whatever it was that Shaman was looking at. I moved as quietly as I could, trying to keep to the shadows. Finally I had a full and unimpeded view of the situation. Things didn't look good.

Jessica had been stripped and bound to the pyramid. Her wrists were tied together and her arms stretched above her head. Her chubby little thighs were spread wide, and her ankles held apart by a long metal rod. Worse still, she was wearing the same blissful, trance-like expression as Shaman's zombies. My thoughts went back to the time she'd been in the power of Stanley Badd's mind control device. Obviously something similar was going on here!

At a signal from Shaman, the chanting stopped and a female acolyte emerged from the shadows. With a start, I realized it was Claire Voyant, the orally obsessed Tarot reader. So she was one of the Servants of Thoth, too! I watched as Claire slipped out of her robe and put her long-nailed fingers to her crotch. She rubbed herself lasciviously a few times, just as I'd seen her do before the Tarot reading. Then she removed Shaman's robes. He stood perfectly still, looking down at her contemptuously. A thick, heavy penis was dangling between his muscular legs. It reached almost to his knees.

Claire raked her sharp fingernails over Shaman's taut body, in long sweeping motions that always ended at his crotch. From shoulders to crotch... chest to crotch... thighs to crotch... buttocks to crotch. Then she knelt in front of him and took his monstrous thing in her mouth.

I visualized her sharply pointed teeth and winced. I was sure she would draw blood. But as I watched, I realized that something weird was happening. It was so weird, that it took several seconds before my brain could interpret it clearly. Claire Voyant wasn't sucking Shaman's penis. His penis was sucking her. It was drawing her whole essence into itself, in a way that was horrible to watch.

When it was over, Claire Voyant had ceased to exist. Shaman's huge phallus jutted up almost vertically, like a thing of stone. He turned towards Jessica, who was still bound helplessly to the pyramid. She smiled at him blissfully -- obviously still a victim of mind control.

I thought back to the cow in the field, and what had happened to it. If I didn't act quickly, the same thing was going to happen to Jessica. Everything depended on me!

20

CONQUERING CHAOS

I fumbled in my pockets for something I could use as a weapon. My fingers closed on the small crystal pyramid that I'd found in the field. It wasn't much, but it would have to do. I threw it at Shaman with all the force I could muster.

My aim wasn't very good. The crystal whizzed past Shaman and hit Jessica on the nose. She blinked in surprise, then peered around to see where the crystal had come from. So did Shaman and his zombies. Suddenly everyone was staring toward my hiding place in the shadows.

Jessica took advantage of the diversion to free herself. She must have used her psychokinesis -- I'd seen her use it before. One moment she was bound hand and foot, the next she was free. She grabbed the pyramid-shaped crystal and turned to Shaman.

Holding the crystal in both hands, Jessica raised it above her head and started to chant a string of strange but carefully articulated words. "K'yarnak phlegethor l'ebumna syha'h n'ghft," she intoned. A sudden flash of energy from the crystal transfixed Shaman. Jessica lowered her arms, then held out her right hand with the fingers spread wide. "The Sign of the Elder Gods be upon thee, Nyarlathotep. Aye, for thou art recognized! Go now, back to the central Chaos from whence thou camest."

With an ear-piercing shriek, the figure of Nik Shaman transformed into the pure energy-form I'd seen in the field. But the energy-thing was much weaker now, and it sank slowly out of sight through the cavern floor. The Servants of Thoth fled for the exit.

I watched as Jessica picked up her clothes and started squeezing back into them. She was whistling quietly to herself. I emerged from my hiding place and went over to her.

She saw me coming. "Frick me!" she said. "You, of all people! What are you doing down here?"

"I thought you needed rescuing," I said, lamely.

She put her hands on her hips. "If there's anyone around here that needs rescuing, it's not me," she said. "I'm a Tantric Elemental -- I can look after myself. You're just... well, you haven't got any psychic powers at all. You haven't even got any non-psychic powers."

"Duh...." I said, as intelligently as I could manage under the circumstances.

"Don't you realize the seriousness of all this?" she asked. "The dangers involved? Nik Shaman was Nyarlathotep, the Crawling Chaos. An ancient, powerful, terrible, terrible menace. Nyarlathotep is an avatar of Azathoth, the personification of ultimate chaos. Chaos that's trying to take over the world. Just like Shaman said in his lecture."

"I knew that," I said. "I mean, I knew that Northalapot was behind it all. Because of the pyramids and the eye. I hadn't quite worked out that he was Nik Shaman, though. But Northalapot was behind the vimanas and Adastra's phoney Air Force people, wasn't he?"

"Yes, he was," Jessica said. "And he was behind the Servants of Thoth, too. And Stanley Badd and his mind control experiments. But they're all free now -- free of Nyarlathotep's influence. It was arrogant of him to meddle in human affairs, and it led to his downfall. It's what put me on his trail. He didn't reckon on having to deal with me."

"You said you were in love with him," I pointed out. "And then you were in some kind of trance, when you were tied to the pyramid."

"That was all an act," Jessica said. "I was in full control all the time. He was planning to have sex with me, and as soon as he entered my body I was going to use my Tantric skills to drain the life out of him. It would have worked too. Then that crystal pyramid appeared out of nowhere, so I decided to use that instead. It wasn't as enjoyable, but it was quicker and less messy."

I went over and picked up the crystal. "This is mine," I said. "I threw it over to you. I found it in a field where Shaman had been mutilating cattle."

Jessica stared at me. "So that was you, was it?" she said. "The pyramid is Nyarlathotep's symbol. It gave me just enough power to deal with him, when I used it in conjunction with the Elder Sign and the mantra of the Old Ones."

"We're a team," I said. "We kicked his ass."

"Yes, we kicked his ass," Jessica agreed. "It won't last, though. He'll regenerate himself, and then someone's going to have to kick his ass all over again."

We left the cavern, and I led the way back to the surface with my flashlight. Finally we climbed up the last of the steps and crawled out of the long-barrow. The sun was up -- we'd been underground for a long time.

We stood blinking for a few seconds. Then Jessica stared at me with her upturned little nostrils. "I still don't understand why you followed me down there," she said. "Why take such a stupid risk?"

"I don't know," I said. "I thought you were in danger, and I wanted to help."

"Oh," said Jessica. She paused for several seconds. "Well, I guess that was kind of sweet, in an empty-headed, dumb-ass sort of way." She gave me a strange look. "You didn't really jerk off Eric Moonblade's dick, did you?"

I was taken aback by the sudden change of subject. "Uh, yes," I said. "Yes, I did do that."

"But why?" She was still staring at me with a strange expression on her face.

"I did it to get back at you," I said. " For saying that mine was too small."

"You're mad," Jessica said. "You're mad, and you're weird, and you're...." She looked totally exasperated. Then she changed the subject again. "You once said I was compensating because I didn't have a penis of my own. You said that I wished I had."

"That's right" I said. "It's true, isn't it?"

"Maybe," Jessica said. She stood for a moment, then turned to walk down the hill.

"Can I have sex with you now?" I asked.

"No," she said.

THE END

Kundalini Conspiracy

Strange things are going on in the town of Blastonbury, and paranormal investigator Byron Bland is determined to get to the bottom of them. UFO sightings, a sinister military experiment, a mysterious cult and a mad scientist are just the start of it.

Byron finds himself embroiled in the weird world of Blastonbury's New Age subculture, and acquires a reluctant ally in the form of Jessica Peace-Lily -- a diminutive, mousy-haired young woman who turns out to be a black-belt Tantric Elemental.

Between them, Byron and Jessica uncover evidence that a long-forgotten but fearsome force is at work -- a force that goes back to the time of ancient Egypt, Atlantis and the lost Indian civilization of Rama.